# WHERE THE MONEY IS

A novel of Las Vegas by

## Ivan G. Goldman

Barricade Books Inc.
New York

Published by Barricade Books Inc.
150 Fifth Avenue
New York, NY 10011

Printed in the United States of America.

Library of Congress Cataloging-in-Publication Data

Goldman, Ivan G.
       Where the money is : a novel of Las Vegas / Ivan G. Goldman.
          p.   cm.
       ISBN 1-56980-052-9
       I. Title.
    PS3557.O3686W44   1995
    813'.54—dc20                                              95-24377
                                                                 CIP

First printing

To everyone who stuck with me long after it stopped making sense, starting with my family — Connie, Jesse, Silvelie, Daniel, and Phyllis Goldman; also, Michael Hamilburg and Joanie Socola of the Mitchell J. Hamilburg Agency, and publisher Lyle Stuart and editor Sandy Stuart.

# CONTENTS

# CHAPTER ONE

# A Change Of Luck

Terry Lasky took an early morning swim in the lap pool at the Mirage Hotel and Casino. As a nonguest, he didn't belong in the water. But in an earlier life as a prosecutor, he'd done a favor for a kid who now worked the morning shift as a lifeguard. Lasky was at least two decades too old to be sneaking into swimming pools, but to ease his shame, the kid always treated him like a favored guest.

Of course, Lasky tipped him. Las Vegas was a town where even lifeguards expected tips. At times Lasky suspected his dentist was angling for a toke after seating him in the chair.

Toweled off and dressed, Lasky headed straight to a blackjack table for one hand at two hundred dollars. The dealer, who could have passed for a high-school cheerleader, busted her hand in three cards, turning Lasky's fifteen into a winner.

After cashing his chips, he walked through the air-conditioned tropical forest, past the torpid white tigers in their art-deco cages, and headed out for breakfast and a newspaper at the Flamingo Hilton across the street.

On the sidewalk, a sturdy beggar with Charlie Manson eyes and a caveman haircut approached. Lasky peeled off two dollars. The man did not thank him. Instead, he glared straight into his eyes and said, "This will change your luck."

"Wait a minute," Lasky said. "I don't want to change my luck."

"This will change your luck!" the beggar commanded, raising the dollar bills into the morning sky like stone tablets. His mad, accusing stare remained fixed on Lasky.

Lasky tried kidding him out of it, but the beggar refused to alter his prophecy. "This will change your luck!" he said a third time.

Lasky feared it was the worst two dollars he ever spent.

❧

The red-eye flight out of O'Hare emptied its usual Saturday morning cargo of hard-core gamblers and generic wastrels—an occasional show girl or sleepy widget sales- man sprinkled among them. The gamblers wore the car- nivorous, expectant look of players about to begin a brand-new round, when everything is still possible. Hear- ing the techno-jangle of the slot machines, their senses squeaked into high gear, and they shot down the airport corridor like a current of field mice.

Waiting just past the gate were two men and a young woman. One of the men wore a droopy mustache, wild, sparse hair, faintly vulgar attire, and the air of a tired man in charge of a bicycle race. This was Max Nettles, a Las

Vegas police lieutenant. Nettles had a street name—Max the Grind, or simply Grinder. Even judges called him Grinder in open court.

The other man, also a detective, was rangy and moved like a breeze through tall grass. There were razor scars on his fingers, relics of a psychopathic boyhood lived out on the streets. He had a long beard pointing down his chest that belonged on a madman or a cabbage commune. It didn't fit the rest of him and made him incongruous anywhere he happened to be, like a chain saw in a string section. They called him Joe the Dentist.

The Dentist had departmental permission for the beard because officially he was listed on the undercover roster. In reality, the infamous Dentist had about as much chance of going undercover in Las Vegas as Wayne Newton. His eyes, made even fiercer by the frame of his Old Testament beard, were those of a football coach or a killer, and the Dentist was nobody's coach. The men stragglers looked away from his terrible eyes as they sneaked glances at the young woman, confident and crisp in a black business suit and perfect white blouse. She was world-class gorgeous, or at least that's what she was paid to be.

But this time out, Grinder noticed, Joanie's celebrated honey skin was a bit overpacked with powder, like she was covering defects. She seemed a little thinner, too, maybe starving herself because perfection was no longer a natural state.

Could be she was about to start the inevitable slide to cocktail waitress or worse. But there was no time to switch girls and anyway, Joanie still had the attitude. It ought to keep her afloat awhile longer.

Grinder could have met with Stalisi after he got settled, but he chose instead to stand at the gate like a schnook. As

Nietzsche put it, there is no fate that can't be overcome by scorn. So when Stalisi charged down the ramp with his gleaming shoes and prematurely cultivated power eyebrows, Grinder took a deep breath of recycled jet fumes and tried to play his part. "Good to see you again, Mr. Stalisi."

Stalisi, who had learned primate dominance in the spiteful outlands of a barely accredited law school, brushed past his three greeters, forcing them to walk along as he advanced towards a limo he seemed to expect somewhere. Finally Grinder managed to stop him for his tags so Joanie could chase down his luggage.

"What's the picture?" Stalisi said, striding forth again.

"You mean on the armored car job," Grinder said.

"No, I flew all the way in to get the Cubs score." Stalisi said it in a flat tone, not exactly scolding, but certainly not friendly, either. He had one of those too-handsome faces you often saw in Vegas, hair and teeth sculpted to anchorman perfection, suit pressed like sheet metal.

As they reached the car, a tired Ford clunker checked out of the departmental motor pool, Joanie showed up with a skycap and Stalisi's two masculine leather bags. Stalisi actually waited for someone to open the rear door for him. Grinder darted forward and yanked it open with just a touch of whimsy. Stalisi paused, staring at him now with a look that had no doubt paralyzed many a secretary.

A worse asshole than he figured, Max the Grind decided. An industrial-strength asshole. A stupid, college-educated little prettyboy wop who even had the audacity to be years younger than Grinder.

As Grinder followed Stalisi into the backseat, Joe started the engine, kicking on the air conditioner. Joanie hung back, not sure whether to get in. She was confused by the coldness of Stalisi, who now pointed a finger at her like she was some kind of bug on the windshield. "What's this?" he said.

"Joanie gives very good reception," Grinder explained. "Bitsy sent her along."

Joanie tried to smile like everything was hunky-dory as the oppressive early-morning sun beat down on her smart black suit.

"Cover story holding up?" Stalisi said, unperturbed by her predicament.

"No problem," Grinder said. "All the stories say the truck was carrying eighteen thousand from the Shangri-la's drop. Bitsy's people, they were ready with the phony paperwork."

"Media's gonna keep swallowing that?" Stalisi asked him.

"They will in this town," Grinder explained. He hated it when people used "media" as a singular noun. Almost everyone did now. The barbarians were past the gate, crapping on everything. "I can't stop reporters coming in from out of town. But I don't think they will. Not enough sex appeal, only eighteen thousand."

"Yeah, we wish it was eighteen thousand," Stalisi said. "Whaddayou know about this bunch of assholes?"

"Might not be a bunch," Grinder said. "Only two pulled the job, and they were both hit. Lost a lot of blood. They dumped the armored truck two minutes after they snatched it. We think they switched into an old van of American manufacture that was seen in the area. Dark green or dark blue. We've got everything closed tight, and we're digging deep. They can't be far."

"You figure to find them?"

"Tonight," Grinder said.

"Why tonight?"

"Because we know where they're headed."

"You know," Stalisi said. Same flat, annoying tone.

"We've got information. Yeah."

"Where they supposed to be?"

"Bob's."

"Bob's?"

"Bob's Beer and Guns," Grinder explained. "A North Vegas joint. They'll be there. The word is it's the only move they've got left."

"Let's go," Stalisi said.

The Dentist obeyed, practically saluting Stalisi as he left Joanie behind like a picked-over melon. The Dentist always remembered his manners with mob guys. They were about the only people he showed any respect, along with other psycho cops and old black men. "Old black men are the only people left who know anything," he'd once told Grinder.

The Dentist took the Tropicana Boulevard ramp west to Paradise Avenue, then proceeded north. He avoided the Strip out of habit, even though there was almost no traffic this early in the day.

The city looked neon tough, cheerfully cruel. A gangster vision of paradise, they used to say. Only now that the corporations had shoved most of the wiseguys out of the way, everything had a more arranged appearance, antiseptic almost. More high rises and fewer traces of street trash.

Despite the calculated touches of comic architecture—the glass pyramid, the seven-story golden lion, and the rest—the tourist sections of Las Vegas somehow had a colder, sleepier look these days, as though this were a kind of desert Zurich. That was part of the city's secret. It had to plunder its visitors matter-of-factly or they might wake up and notice the well-manicured fingers going through their pockets. Las Vegas was an island of certainty functioning smoothly even as a dark centrifugal force tore great portions of American territory off their foundation and each year the afternoon freaks on Donahue and Oprah got freakier.

Meanwhile, beyond the towering new casinos, beyond the storybook castles and man-made volcanos, sat mile after mile of vicious stinkholes where cops gave each other directions by explaining the location was two blocks north of yesterday's gang rape and a block east of that severed arm from last month. The casinos sucked dollars from the slums like atom-powered Hoovers, imposing an added tax on the poor that made them even more angry and hard to control.

Each year it grew tougher to protect the suckers from Cedar Rapids who strolled around their preserve like fat wallets on skinny legs. Harder and harder to fence them off as exclusive game for the casinos.

But like the beautiful Joanie he left back on the airport curb, all the calculated efforts, all the patchwork ironies of Vegas were details of no use to Stalisi.

He smelled sweet, neat, and scrubbed even after a three-hour plane ride. Must have freshened up just before landing. Probably changed shirts, too. Excessive gestures, really. And if he cared so much about his appearance, why leave a gem like Joanie gleaming on the asphalt? There ought to be some purpose beyond vanity.

Could be he was gay, but more likely Stalisi was just another hypertense Grasping Urban Professional. To him, sex was a scheduled activity, like racquetball. This guy was all business and out of context, striving within the metallic confines of an unexamined life that Plato had correctly labeled not worth living twenty-five hundred years before this mob-connected shit never thought of it.

"So you don't really know where the stash is, do you?" Stalisi said.

"With any luck at all, we'll have the hijackers tonight," Grinder said. "And it's my guess they'll know where the cargo is. In my experience, people who steal three million, they generally remember where they put it."

"You know," Stalisi said, "some people in Chicago, they're not happy with you right now, Nettles."

"You can call me Grinder. Or Lieutenant. Whichever you like."

"Well, Lieutenant, the thing is, my uncle, he's paying you all this money, and you let some bozos rip us off anyway. If they were bozos."

"First off, I don't have any deal with your uncle, who pays me nothing," Grinder said. "My deal's with Bitsy, like always. Second, it—"

"Look—" Stalisi interrupted.

"Listen, to me," Grinder told him.

Stalisi raised his power eyebrows a notch.

"Second, the deal doesn't cover hijackings. You're supposed to look after your own shit, understand? You got a problem? Okay, we'll lend a hand. But that doesn't mean you can go blaming us. Third, you seem to be hinting that maybe I had something to do with this caper. You're way off base, understand? You ask around, and you'll see just how stupid that remark was."

"What remark you talking about?"

"'If they were bozos,' you said. That one. See, you were implying two things—one, I'm a thief, and two, I'm no bozo. But you should know the score before you open your mouth, okay?"

Stalisi didn't reply. A surrender of sorts.

"Because I am a bozo," Grinder said. "Right, Joe?"

"Absolutely. He's a bozo," Joe the Dentist said.

"Thank you." Grinder turned back to Stalisi. "But I didn't rip off your sorry-ass armored truck. Armed robbery's not what I do. But forget about that. The main thing is, I don't welsh on a deal, understand? Never. Your uncle, Mr. Venassio, maybe he understands that. But if he doesn't, I'll be happy to explain it myself, and you can find your own cargo. I got other cases to work on."

"Look, I'm not accusing you of ripping off the cargo," Stalisi said. Grinder watched Joe smile in the rearview mirror. Maybe he sucked up to mob guys, but he was still his partner.

"Good, then let's forget about it," Grinder said. "Maybe I misinterpreted."

"You got to understand, everything's crazy. I came down here middle of the night, no sleep."

"You musta been asleep back at the airport, turning away Joanie like that," Grinder said. "You should never be in such a hurry to throw away pretty women. They could get scarce someday." He'd heard that line before, hadn't he? *Casablanca*. That's it. The cop said it to Bogart. They might become scarce, the cop said. But Stalisi wouldn't know from *Casablanca*. This mob nephew was a perfect example of what happened when wiseguys made it in America. They moved to the suburbs and sired kids like this. Kids who weren't tough, weren't smart either. No wonder they got ripped off.

"Not in Chicago," Stalisi said.

"What?"

"Foxes," Stalisi said. "They're not scarce where I come from either."

"That's nice to hear," Grinder said. "We got our share around here, too. We get the best." Jesus, he sounded like the chamber of commerce. Finest hookers in three time zones.

After his promotion, people told him he should start dressing like a police lieutenant instead of a lounge-act emcee. Might be worth it if it would impress weasels like this one, keep them from trying to bite him on the neck. But everything would go easier now if he let the little nephew kiss and make up.

"Hey Joe, what the hell kind of fuckup outfit is that you got on?" Grinder said.

"It's what all the fuckups are wearing this season," Joe the Dentist replied. Joe never forgot his lines. The three of them had a good insincere laugh.

# CHAPTER TWO

# In the Dark With the Dead

All his life Berkeley followed advice he knew stunk.
Just one of those things. It seemed he always knew
what to do, but he'd end up listening to somebody else instead. Sometimes anybody else. But this time he listened to
his own heart, which told him to forget the original plan
and follow the arroyo to the abandoned post office, a place
he'd never lost a cargo. And he was right on the money.
Lost them all miles back, circling around each other in the
dark like blue bumpkins. If he'd taken the back road into
the bottling plant, he'd probably be just another dead
chump by now.

Must have checked his watch three thousand times the
last twenty-one hours, sitting in the dark with a dead man.
Now it was time. He turned on the headlights and stepped
out of the van. The dull pain in his left side turned white
hot, just for a second, and he let out a cry in the solitude. It
didn't help. The wound was bleeding less now, but he
wasn't sure anymore how serious it was. He still couldn't

remember which side the liver was on. If it was on the right, what was on the left? He'd pop another red, but he couldn't remember when he'd swallowed the last one. Everything was slowing down and speeding up at the same time, like he was surrounded by fire and ice.

It seemed like the whole time down here he'd been working up the nerve just to pull Moulin's body out of the seat beside him. It ought to be a simple task. Like jumping out of a plane. You just closed your eyes and did it.

He circled around, opened the double doors of the van and climbed in back to take a last deep breath of that dreamy sweet money smell. Nice old unmarked bills bundled in stacks of twenties and hundreds that fought the lonely dread washing over him. He grabbed a short stack of twenties, tore off the binder, and stuck them in his jeans.

He threw down the makeshift ramp and removed the tarp covering his Harley. Then he wheeled it out of the van, tossed the ramp back inside, and closed the double doors.

As fast as he could, he dragged Moulin's bullet-chewed body out of the passenger seat. It was worse than he imagined. Moulin hadn't died easy. Breathing hard, he leaned his friend's corpse against a tire without looking at the eyes and returned to the front seat. He removed his sleeveless denim jacket and carefully put it on over his T-shirt, covering the wound. Stuffing shells in his pocket, he grabbed one of the sawed-off shotguns and slung it inside his jacket.

He reached inside and turned off the headlights. Then he wheeled his motorcycle over to the freight elevator and took it up one level to the enormous freight area on the ground floor, where it smelled faintly of old shit.

His wound made everything more intense. The stink, the loneliness, the deadness all around. Shafts of desert starlight trickled through great banks of broken windows and skylights into the huge abandoned space. Pigeons rustled and cooed. Under his feet he could feel layers of Styrofoam bits, crumpled cans, broken bottles, rags, hairpins, cigarette butts, pop-tops, and who knew what else? The Harley gleamed incongruously.

In the starlight, his night vision acute from the hours of darkness in the cellar, he could almost make out the posters on the walls. Mail early; use Overnight Express; use zip codes. Would have been nice to have a zip code again, live in one of those nice new garden apartments where a civil service flunky stuck mail in his box six days a week. Have a nice stereo, check out cuties at the pool. He didn't need much. Just more than he had.

One of his professors used to say it didn't matter if you had to buy your tires out of junkyards. Just being educated gave you a fuller life. Yeah, sure.

Berkeley sent the empty elevator back down to the basement, and the metal gratings closed automatically over the top. If anyone looked around up here, they probably wouldn't even recognize it as an elevator.

Moulin's going to stink up the loot, but this was the best way. Nothing for anyone to find. No body, no van, no loot. Just mystery, and maybe a little blood.

With a clasp knife, he snipped off a length of wire leading from his portable generator to the wall button. He threw the wire in a corner, then removed the distributor cap from the generator and slipped it in his pocket.

He mounted the Harley. When it started on the second kick, he felt a familiar wave of confidence work its way through the saddle into his body. He steered across the floor, down the loading dock, and into the desert night toward the city.

# Chapter Three

# Bob's Beer and Guns

At Bob's Beer and Guns, Terry Lasky, sitting at a corner table, heard the latest on the hijacking moments before the house dealer dealt him his first three cards in a pot-limit game of seven-card stud. They were all fives. Lasky was not quite handsome, not quite young, and up till now, he wasn't winning.

"You're trying to look into my eyes again," said Lasky, gazing from his three fives into the face of a player showing an ace. The player was a sour-faced mugger on a poker break, yet another drifter who'd wandered into Vegas seeking work, lost his grubstake at the tables, and stuck around to get it back any way he could.

"So what do you see?" Lasky said.

The mugger, always deliberate, took his time replying. "A loser, I hope," he said finally.

"You know, I think we've been trying to outsmart each other too long," Lasky said. "Now we're triple-thinking each other."

"Speak for yourself," said the only woman at the table. "I'm still trying to master single-think."

"Then where'd all those chips come from?" said the mugger.

"Triple thinkers, mostly," she said.

The woman sat behind the table's largest pile, her chips stacked in neat columns. Lasky had read somewhere this was a tip-off. Precise stacks meant a precise player. But he wasn't sure about the next step. Should he play precisely against such a player? Or try to throw her off with goofball strategies?

"Are you betting or jabbering?" said Bags, an exmacroeconomist on parole. Always an impatient player, he was only half-kidding.

"I'm merely trying to disguise the value of my cards," Lasky said.

The mugger looked straight at Lasky, who saw a dead, pitiless expression that could have belonged to a sex shop cashier. "Okay, let's cut the bullshit. How good *is* your hand?"

"Too early to tell," Lasky said, first suppressing laughter, then letting it out as he opened with a bet.

The ex-macroeconomist raised, and six of the seven players paid for a fourth card.

"Hey," the mugger said as the dealer spun out more cards. "Where would you take a truck loaded with mob money?"

"They'll never get the chance to enjoy it," said another player. This player took credit for bringing the word in off the street that last night's hijacking was no nickel-and-dime eighteen thou caper like the TV said. The armored truck apparently was hauling mob millions. Nobody seemed to know how many millions or what the loot was doing in the vehicle, but everyone loved this delicious story.

"Every dago in town's gonna have their ears to the ground," the player said. "They'll get it back, all right. Might take a bit, but they'll get it back."

This player owned a local chain of transmission shops, sported big watches and cars, and frequently escorted lazy young women with big teeth and too much perfume who chewed gum, smoked cigarettes, and sipped sugary cocktails all at the same time, all the while listening attentively to the transmission king while he stated the obvious, over and over.

"Mob guys," he said, "they don't have to read anybody their rights."

Paroled economist Bags carefully scratched the top of his head. He was one of those deflated souls who plastered spaghetti-length hairs from one side of his bald head to the other. "Looks like a mess of greasy kite string," a shrimpy crack whore once told him from the bottom of her whisky glass. "You are what you are, man. Face it." Leaving him mute and deflated. You are what you are.

Lasky knew the head scratch was a nervous tell, a road map to his bankroll.

❧

Outside Bob's Beer and Guns, Berkeley pulled his bike into the littered sand lot and killed the engine. A Pakistani vendor tried without much enthusiasm to sell him a brightly painted statuette of Elvis splayed on a cross. Ignoring him, Berkeley gulped down two more reds. He strode past a line of cabbies towards the sounds of the reggae sextet inside.

Cabbies liked Bob's. Its customers, mostly locals, were

less likely to blame the driver for the way the cards fell. One of Berkeley's old girlfriends who dealt blackjack likened the job to working on a firing squad. "You're hated by the people you're paid to shoot," she said, "and hated even more by the people who pay you to do it."

Inside, Berkeley moved casually past the sinewy black bouncer with most of one ear missing. At the gun counter, Bob Tangeli, the proprietor, sat in a wheelchair showing revolvers to a couple of homely yuppies. The yuppie woman sighted down the barrel of a German model. "Is this any quicker than a single action?" she asked.

"Is the pope black?" answered Tangeli. He blew a tuft of gray-blond hair away from his eyes.

"No," the yuppie man said. "The pope is Polish."

"Whatever," Bob Tangeli said.

"Where's Lasky?" Berkeley asked him.

Tangeli, who didn't miss much, gazed at Berkeley a long time. Too long. Could the shotgun be showing? Berkeley brazened it out, waiting. "Playing stud," Tangeli finally told him.

Berkeley made his way along the wall opposite the long, scarred bar and beneath the huge abstract painting done mostly in shades of blue that perhaps depicted a lonesome street. The Rasta sextet took a break, and the musicians filed past Berkeley in the other direction. They were a savvy, capable bunch—missing some teeth.

Berkeley was no regular here, but he'd cut some meth deals at the bar and was familiar with the crowded, barn-sized joint that was a second home to grifters, dreamers, dealers, waitresses, even an occasional casino executive. Of course, it was technically illegal to sell guns inside a bar. But somehow, no doubt after paying the correct *mordida* to the correct authorities, Tangeli had convinced them to sanction a folding plywood separator as the required boundary between the gun shop and the bar operation.

Two or three drinkers nodded greetings to Berkeley. He ignored them.

There was Lasky, playing cards almost directly beneath a display case on the wall that contained an innocuous brown T-shirt that Tangeli maintained had once been worn by Bob Dylan.

Berkeley thought he might be bleeding again. He wanted to do this fast, then score some downers before he figured his next move. One of those 20-milligram turbos should do it—kill the pain and fight back against all those reds racing around in his blood.

Lasky didn't look much like a government attorney anymore, but it was worth a shot. His only shot, far as he could see.

Just as he was dealt his fourth card, Lasky saw the shaggy, possibly looney biker hovering over him, wanting something. Lasky knew him from someplace. He looked down and read the card—the fourth five. He felt a sweet buzz rise from his toes to the top of his tickled head. "Pair of fives high," announced the dealer, reading the board.

Lasky shoved in three red chips for bait.

"Bet's fifteen," said the dealer. It was now up to Pastor Pinky, who contemplated his cards with little gray eyes, like old tarnished dimes. He took his time a lot. It rattled some players, something he didn't mind at all.

In the spare indoor light of Bob's, Pinky, a man of indeterminate age, had one of those feathery honky complexions found on Alabama hardware clerks or certain Irish priests. Lasky knew the face was a cutting ground for plastic surgeons, the stretched layers of skin carefully blanketed with a fine powder and topped by silken razor-cut hair that shined yellow white, complementing the glare of his lightweight suit. The doctors had chiseled Pinky's formerly bulbous nose into a sweet Grace Kelly nub. But, of course, they could do nothing with his hands, which looked like they belonged inside a casket.

Pinky traveled with an entourage tonight—two Stepford Wife hookers and his bodyguard.

"You know, I like you, Terry," Pastor Pinky told Lasky. "But case you haven't noticed, this here's a poker table, and at a poker table, I'd slip a rattlesnake in your pocket and then ask you for a match." The two Stepford hookers tried to laugh, but they were bad actors. Pinky tossed in thirty, raising the action.

"Jesus, I must have heard you say that a hundred times," ex-macroeconomist Bags said, blinking straight ahead. "Why is it that all good ole boys think you want to hear their same sorry-ass quips over and over again? You know? Cousins just shouldn't marry cousins. The French got Toulouse Lautrec, and we end up with Gomer fucking Pyle."

Pastor Pinky's smile vanished, but his tarnished-dime eyes remained cheerful, giving him a suddenly sinister look. "You musta been real popular in the penitentiary, Professor, smart mouth like yours. Bet you had lots a nice boyfriends." Pinky turned and addressed his hookers. "Goddamned rat-faced, baldheaded sonofabitch," he said. They giggled and his smile returned.

Bags muttered something unintelligible.

Lasky, not interested in their bickering, tried with all his being to mask the emotional cartwheels he was doing behind his four fives. It looked like this biker standing over him was about to tell him something. But then the waitress did first, storming through the tables, swinging her pregnant belly like a sledgehammer. "I got a table full a turkeys trying to pay in bogus chips," she announced to Lasky. "From the Rabbit's Foot."

Lasky could only hope his voice wouldn't betray his hand. "Damn," he replied, maybe too carefully. "You're positive they're no good?"

"The chips or the turkeys?" the waitress asked him.

"I meant the chips, but I guess both."

"Cap already called the Rabbit. They said the chips figure to be from some old promotion or something. As for the turkeys, I wouldn't ask any of'm to watch my purse, I can tell you that."

Everyone else called the bet, and the action went back to Lasky.

"What's the tab?" he asked her.

"Thirty-three bucks," the waitress said.

Lasky studied his cards, tried to appear like a loser hoping to see them improve. Finally the biker leaned over. "I gotta talk to you," he said.

Lasky looked up, trying to remember this guy's name. Nothing doing. But he recognized him now from an old case. He looked desperate that time, too—a petty tweak dealer who'd known enough about a stolen car ring to fink his way out of being prosecuted in a case that had holes in it anyway. Before that, he'd been a cargo handler at the airport until a surveillance camera caught him going through suitcases. It was amazing how some people stepped squarely and accurately from the middle of one turd to another. Like the Palestinians Henry Kissinger described, they never missed an opportunity to miss an opportunity.

"You playing?" the transmission king said to Lasky.

"Let him do his job," said ex-macroeconomist Bags, who clearly loathed spending any time with this uncircumcised Philistine transmission king who somehow held his own at stud.

Lasky felt sorry for Bags, the poor, tormented embezzler schnook. Like every con Lasky ever knew, Bags had only one real regret—getting caught. From sex monsters to junk-bond kings, they all shared the same gene of innocence. If only their old man had stuck around. If only the cops'd go after the real bad guys. If only—the antithesis of existential thought. They were never responsible for their own lives. Except when they got lucky.

"You been raised," the dealer told Lasky.

Lasky threw in two twenty-five-dollar green chips. "Raise," he said.

"Well?" the waitress said.

"You know the drill," Lasky told her. "Have Cap handle it. If they don't fork over, tell him to—"

"Take their shoes," she answered for him. The waitress started to leave. Lasky stopped her.

"Martha?"

"Mmmmm?"

"Tell him to do it quietly this time."

"Not like last time," she said.

"Not like last time," Lasky said.

She plunged past tables and customers towards the bouncer. The biker leaned closer again. "I really gotta talk to you," he said in a half-whisper.

"Look around. I work in a saloon now," Lasky told the biker. Berkeley. That was his name, Berkeley. The last Lasky had heard, he was growing compost piles out in the boonies. "I'm not looking for cases, okay?"

"Fuck cases," the biker said. "This is business."

"Just give me a minute," Lasky said. "These people are beating me into the ground here."

Everyone met Lasky's raise except the transmission king, who threw his cards down in disgust. When Pastor Pinky raised the bet, Lasky just called, hoping his display of doubt would draw money into the pot later.

The dealer dealt the five remaining players a fifth card. Pastor Pinky showed a pair of kings now, but looking puzzled, he checked. So did everyone else. This was curious, but Lasky went along. Let them try to catch some cards.

"Hey," said the transmission king. "I go in, everybody raises. I fold, the next round's free. What is this?"

"It's what we all agreed to do," said one of the players.

"Cut the shit, willya?" said the transmission king.

"It's true," said another player.

"Nobody likes you," said the woman player.

"You're bullshitting me, right?" said the transmission king. He turned to Lasky. "They're bullshitting me, right?"

Meanwhile, Berkeley wouldn't go away. "I need your help, man," he said in a whispery voice, almost whining now.

"Sure, we were bullshitting you," the mugger told the transmission king. "Trust us."

On the sixth card, Pastor Pinky caught an ace on top of his two kings and tossed in a hundred-dollar chip. "Time to see who's serious," he said. Pinky would never let go of this pot now. And the play was to Lasky. But before he could move, Berkeley clutched him high on the arm and squeezed. Lasky wrenched his arm away.

"We're trying to play stud here," a player objected.

"Codpick's running the office now," Lasky told Berkeley. "I'll give you his number after this hand, okay?"

"You gotta help," Berkeley said. "You helped me once before, remember? When you were U.S. attorney."

"Assistant. I was an *assistant* U.S. attorney," Lasky corrected him. "I didn't even run the football pool." Lasky called and raised a hundred.

Two players called.

"What the hell you got along with those two measly little fives?" Pinky said. "I thought you shills're supposed to just throw in antes, not make life so damn miserable for the paying customers." He studied his hole cards some more, then looked around the board carefully. "Well," he said finally, "you got me confused all right. But when I get confused, it makes me mad." He reraised two hundred.

"Codpick's dead, man," Berkeley said.

"What are you talking about?" Lasky said.

"Codpick's dead. He croaked four, five weeks ago."

"Codpick? Leslie Codpick is dead?" Lasky said. "Damn, what killed him?"

"I dunno," Berkeley said. "Cancer, I think. But look, man, I know you quit. But you're still the guy I need." He snapped a quick look over his shoulder, as though daring others to listen. "Let's do this somewhere else, understand?"

"I understand you don't understand," Lasky told him. "I'm the worst possible person you could choose if you want help from the U.S. attorney's office. Walk in with Charlie Manson, they'll make you a better deal."

Lasky always felt tricked when he learned about someone's death after an interval of weeks or months or years. You went around assuming everyone was frozen in the last circumstance you saw them in. But people just never got in touch to tell you they're dead.

Codpick had been a hard-drinking would-be raconteur,

self-absorbed and lazy. He used to massage typists and sec-
retaries on the back, play with their bra straps if they had
them. It was rarely found amusing. Another third-rater
with just enough connections to make people around him
miserable. But it was still unsettling to hear of his death.
How many other dead Codpicks were walking around live
in Lasky's perception?

Berkeley's patience looked about gone, as though everything was conspiring against him just a little faster than he
could handle. For an instant, Lasky believed this nut was
about to assault him. But the moment passed like a vague
morning dream across the biker's grizzled face.

"You're right," Berkeley said, his voice too loud now.
"Dumb idea coming here. Dumb. I just—I don't know. I just
figured—" He looked like a farmer in foreclosure. "But I remembered that other time, the cops, they weren't going to
keep the deal. You stood up for me. You didn't have to, but
you stood up for me and stuff. For the deal, remember? It
was you saved my ass. And I can't do this all alone, not
with this—I need help. I had a long time to think it through.
You're the one."

Pastor Pinky, suddenly aware of something, sprang to
his feet. "Let me help," he implored Berkeley.

And just like that, the biker took a deep breath and
pulled the sawed-off from under his jacket, aiming it at the
pink-cheeked pastor. "Back off, you little faggot bastard!"
Berkeley lunged at Lasky, grabbing him around the head in
a kind of desperation headlock and using the leverage to
steady himself. His skin had a salty smell to it. Lasky's ear
was bending in the headlock, and he squirmed to free it as
the world around him took this quick wrong turn. Somebody screamed. Customers jostled one another, trying to
back away.

"Okay," Lasky heard Pastor Pinky say. "Okay." Lasky, caught in a macabre dance with the biker, thought he saw Pinky's bodyguard pull a semiautomatic pistol and level it in his direction. He sensed someone coming his way as others scattered and sought cover. Berkeley pressed his lips to Lasky's bent ear and whispered, whispered carefully as though he had plenty of time. Then he shoved Lasky away, and Lasky remembered the beggar from yesterday morning, and the beggar's command: "This will change your luck."

"Don't shoot him!" someone yelled. Don't shoot who? Lasky hit the deck as Berkeley swiveled his sawed-off and fired. Somebody slammed into the table. A pistol went off—many shots in a quick, steady pattern, probably eight or nine times.

Everyone stayed still a few moments, as though posing for a photograph. Lasky recognized Grinder now. He was the first one up. When did he come in?

"Dammit, I said don't shoot him!" Grinder shouted. Berkeley was down in a heap. One of the players was torn to pieces, probably by the shotgun blast. Grinder was already going through Berkeley's pockets, wiping blood on the dead man's clothes as he went. He found a wad of bills which he held up to the light, then placed on the body. He handed a key ring to his partner, Joe the Dentist. The Dentist, holstering his gun, was calm as a lily pond.

"Anybody see what this guy drove up with?" Grinder announced. Everyone looked at him dumbly. "I said did anybody see what this guy drove? How'd he get here?" Still no answer.

"Joe," Grinder said to his partner, "see if those keys fit anything out there." The Dentist shouldered his way through the crowd towards the door.

One of the players bent among the scattered chips and cards to pick up something. "This is a crime scene!" Grinder shouted, stopping him.

Lasky rose, relieved to be alive. At the same time a familiar uneasiness took hold, one he hadn't felt for many years. "Goddammit it!" he shouted. "Where's my hand?" A couple players laughed, breaking the tension of death and near-death. "I had four fives!" Lasky shouted. "I had four fucking fives!"

"Sure," said the mugger. "And the check's in the mail, right?" Lasky kneeled. He searched the mess on the floor without touching anything.

"Leave that shit alone," Grinder said.

Lasky shook his head. "Four fives," he said quietly, then stood up again, pointing. "There's two of them."

Grinder, standing over the body of Berkeley, asked no one in particular, "What was his name?"

"Funny, he never passed out business cards," the woman player said. She looked ready to cry.

"They called him Berkeley," somebody said.

"Berkeley?"

"I heard he had a . . .whaddyacall it . . .a football scholarship there. Long time ago, I guess. But he got into some kind of trouble."

Someone addressed Lasky. "What did he tell you? When he whispered?" Lasky turned to see an aggressively handsome young man, his dark hair combed back carefully, as though he were modeling for an *Esquire* ad. "What did he tell you?" handsome repeated.

The Dentist returned from the parking lot and whispered something to Grinder and handsome, who must be with them. But handsome didn't look much like a cop.

"I said what did he tell you?" handsome asked again.

"Who's your friend?" Lasky asked Grinder.

"Mr. Stalisi is an insurance investigator," Grinder said.

Lasky appraised him, and it all began to make sense. Insurance as in Cosa Nostra Insurance. "You're awfully nice to him," Lasky observed. "Must be a pretty important company. Aren't you going to call homicide about these two dead guys? Or you want us to?"

"You let us worry about that," Grinder said. "Don't go talking lawyer talk now, Terry. We're just simple policemen asking simple questions."

"Lawyer? This guy's no lawyer," Joe the Dentist said. "He's a shill."

"If you guys can call yourselves police officers, then I guess I can call myself a lawyer," Lasky said.

"Why don't I question him?" the Dentist said to Grinder. Calm, determined. Like he was about to crack open a clam. The Stalisi character looked on approvingly.

Grinder and the Dentist were officially assigned to the Organized Crime Intelligence Division. A murky assignment that burst with irony and left them ample time to run errands for their real bosses, organized criminals.

"Hold it, hold it, hold it," Bob Tangeli said, wheeling himself forward. He squinted through the smoke of a cigarette between his lips. The sound and sight of him had a calming effect. Something about paraplegics made others thoughtful. Also, most of the nerves and muscles on the left side of his mouth were dead, so he spoke in a Dead End Kids delivery, making everything he said seem less than serious. "Let's take it easy," said Tangeli, who knew all about it.

"Grinder, we're trying to run a business here, and you're leaving bodies around," Tangeli said. "Can't you at least cover them up so our customers won't be so distracted from the slot machines?"

Grinder smiled, choosing to ignore bouncer Cap, a silent, lean presence who casually cradled a shotgun behind Bob's chair. An ex-prizefighter, Cap had been collecting aluminum cans in a shopping cart when Bob plucked him off the street with a job offer. Doubtless he would wrestle grizzlies to protect his boss. But with an unspoken gesture, Bob sent him back to watch the front door.

A couple uniformed cops rushed in from outside, and Grinder had them isolate the crime scene with yellow streamers. Acting like a cop now, he started making calls and sorting out witnesses.

No one seemed to know the dead gambler. He was what experienced players referred to as a "calling station"—a timid player who folded too late and rarely raised. A patsy. Now the ultimate patsy. He looked about twenty-four. The age of a squad sergeant or a platoon commander, Lasky realized. Even dead, he looked scared. "When your number's up, it's up," somebody volunteered.

"Bullshit," Lasky muttered. As though this poor bastard, had he dodged the shotgun blast, would have been struck down tonight by some errant microbe. Bullshit. There weren't any numbers. The kid could have seen a movie tonight and maybe lived another fifty years. It's what made life so terrifying. Decisions. Decisions and all those random horrors that circled the planet like killer mosquitoes.

More cops arrived. They took a lot of photographs and questioned everybody, but barely spoke to Lasky. They acted almost like he wasn't there. Finally the morgue people showed up. They carted away Berkeley and the kid and let the two Salvadoran janitors mop up the blood and put everything back together.

The patrons returned to their games, their beers, their musings, their own ribbons of time. And every so often, they cast curious glances at Lasky, the last man to speak with Berkeley.

The remaining players bickered a solid ten minutes over how to divide the spilled chips. Finally Tangeli adjudicated the matter. Lasky, playing as though there were justice in the world, found some, winning the next pot with a pair of queens.

Out in the parking lot, where Grinder filled in Stalisi, four frightened-looking young men charged out the door of Bob's—minus their shoes.

# CHAPTER FOUR

# Eating Dog

Next day Lasky woke with gradual discomfort as the Nevada sun cooked his trailer roof. It was just before noon when he entered the shower. He knew life was about to get more complicated. He waited until he was dressed before checking his drawer, hoping he'd remembered the game wrong or miscounted somehow. No. He went through his pockets twice. Nothing.

It's one thing to gamble away your money at night, quite another the next day. A different you now wondering how the previous you, the one who'd been in charge last night, could have been such a chump. There was a message from Snapper on his machine. She had bankrolled his game, so the humiliation wasn't even finished. He couldn't face calling her back just now.

At least he was well rested, had tumbled immediately to sleep like always, despite the lost chips, the message from Berkeley, all of it. Years ago, Lasky knew men who could sleep untroubled after being half-fried inside an armored vehicle during the course of their day. "Least I ain't well done," a kid once told him. "Easy over, maybe, but I mean, what's a little hair singed off your balls? We'll get 'em tomorrow, right? Less they get us. Har." And sure enough, they got him.

Lasky remained baffled that Berkeley had searched him out, confided in a man who barely recalled his name. But his reasons were something Berkeley never had time to explain. Did he want to make a deal with the government? The mob? Did he still believe he could get away somehow? Maybe he wasn't sure himself. Clearly he was overwhelmed and alone. So he just whispered and died, relieving himself of the burden. Passing it elsewhere.

Berkeley was exactly the kind of humorless prick Lasky made it a point to avoid. A ding for sure. Lasky remembered the file. He was a kid who could have coasted through life on scholarship. But in his senior year at the university, for reasons known only to him, he shoplifted a bottle of vodka under his jacket, was spotted, and crashed through a store window. Bloodied, he sailed into the arms of two cops, ending his student athlete scam and launching his miserable nickel-and-dime rap-sheet existence over ten bucks worth of vodka.

Lasky grabbed his emergency hundred-dollar bill from the drawer. He was hungry but had to get going. He headed out the door into the relentless sunlight surrounding his trailer, which squatted, uninvolved, along with two others behind an abandoned service station.

Lasky knew the Arab word for this kind of morning air: *hamsin*. A word he'd learned in Israel. When the air was gritty and gray with sand, when there was a hot stillness that settled uneasily in your liver like bad booze, it was called a *hamsin*. Around Vegas it was called just another day.

Lasky nodded to a neighbor, a young Chinese man who sat at a card table under a canvas canopy, clacking pai gow tiles with another oriental.

"Wait," the neighbor said. "We got some lunch left."

"Thanks, but I'm in a hurry," Lasky replied.

Lasky and the neighbor did favors for each other. Neither could remember the other's name.

"No problem, eat fast," the neighbor said. "Otherwise I throw it out." Terry doubted this, but he accepted the favor.

The other player smiled as the neighbor disappeared into his trailer. He had cultivated one three-inch fingernail on an index finger, and it was hard not to stare at it as he emerged moments later and passed Lasky a plate of food and a fork. Without preliminaries, Lasky tore into chucks of meat with a basil sauce poured over rice. The two players resumed their game, slamming down tiles, cursing, grunting, chuckling.

After awhile the neighbor looked up and addressed Lasky. "You know what you eat?" He and his buddy both smiled at Lasky now. A big joke of some kind. When his neighbor smiled, you could see all his teeth, even the bottom row.

"Tell me," Lasky said.

"You want to know now," the neighbor said, teasing.

"Absolutely."

"Dog," the neighbor said.

Lasky nodded thoughtfully, "Give me the recipe sometime, okay?" he said, then shoved the last forkful into his mouth.

The two players burst into laughter, a rollicking almost frantic storm of hilarity that rolled up from the knees, brought tears to their eyes, and turned into the kind of laughing siege these two would want to remember later, sometime when they didn't feel like laughing. What the hell, Lasky couldn't help himself—he laughed, too. So of course they laughed even harder.

When Lasky left, they were in a stop-and-start mode, new waves of hilarity building, dying, building again. The neighbor had never kidded with him before, which made him suspect he'd really eaten dog. He wished he had time to brush his teeth again.

Lasky was afoot. His car, old enough to be bar mitzvahed, sat back in Bob's parking lot with a scorched starter under the hood. He cut through the abandoned gas pumps to emerge onto a thoroughfare lined with several bars, and discos, side-by-side like townhouses. Two of the joints blasted mindless disco dreck from speakers aimed onto the street. They competed in a mad cacophony that could drive a dharma monk to Valium.

Near the end of the street, Lasky came upon the traveling soup kitchen run by Rabbi Ike and the Reverend Mike.

"Alsatian pate, endive and tomato salad, two kinds of pasta, and venison roasted over a charcoal spit," the rabbi, a black-coated Chassid, called out to Lasky. "And we got maybe a little apricots and cream."

Lasky cursed himself for eating the possibly canine meal. Also for not having a dollar bill to slip Ike and Mike. "Thanks, I've eaten," he told the rabbi.

Less than three years ago the rabbi's small flock of Chassidic followers made all the necessary arrangements to leave the San Fernando Valley of Los Angeles and settle on the West Bank of the Jordan. A week before departure, his wife, no doubt frazzled by the impending journey, tried to exit the Ventura Freeway too late, when her car was already shooting past the ramp. She hit the brake and cut across two lanes, and she and their three small children were crushed by an eighteen-wheeler.

The rabbi buried his family and disappeared. He probably never found out whether any of his congregation made the journey. Months later he turned up in Las Vegas to await the Messiah among the city's surplus store of wicked and broken souls.

Somewhere along the line, he teamed up with the grumpy Reverend Mike, a Pentacostal minister who'd been found wanting by a number of ex-congregations in south Texas. Both saw the cruel back streets, gaming tables, and fleshpots of Las Vegas as signs of the Messiah's imminent approach. But the Reverend Mike expected Jesus to return, and Rabbi Ike was confident this would be the Anointed One's first trip to Earth. Each eagerly awaited the day he could tell the other I told you so. Meanwhile they worked in near-perfect symbiosis, gleaning food from mysterious sources and feeding noninstitutional gourmet meals to all comers at unannounced locations around the city.

Rabbi Ike scrounged up the ingredients, and the Reverend Mike directed the kitchen. "He just read a few books," the rabbi explained to anyone who asked. "He says anybody who can read can cook. There's no mystery."

After just a couple of years on the scene, Ike and Mike were already a Vegas landmark. On any given day Willie Nelson or Tony Bennett might stop by to make a donation and eat a delicious stand-up meal.

Lasky passed under the marquee of a large, theaterlike building advertising live nudes. Outside the cashier's cage, he watched a bouncer expertly smash a man in the teeth, once. Another man, a strolling vendor of antitheft devices for steering wheels, addressed the struck man, now crumpled in a fetal ball on the asphalt. "I tole ya," the vendor said. "I tole ya."

Parked across the street, outside a cowboy bar, a man hung upside down out the driver's door of a rusted, sand-caked pickup. He was throwing up. The vomit spewed past his eyes. His arms dangled like a doll's.

Lasky turned the corner and came to a bus stop. But he had no idea which buses went where, and he was in no mood to learn. Times like these he felt himself a stranger in this city which only played at welcoming strangers.

High, straight wisps of clouds hung over the blue-white sky as three apparent humans totally covered in black bags stood like sentinels on the corner. Muslim women? There was no end to the surprises lurking on the back streets of American-Way-to-Play Las Vegas.

The three figures barely moved, making him uncomfortable. They must have peepholes. It was like standing in front of a one-way mirror without knowing who watched from the other side. He walked a block west and hailed a cab, pulling open the oven-hot handle of a polished Nissan.

Stepping into a refrigerated taxi interior, Lasky told the driver, a wiry Third Worlder with a Pachuco tattoo at the base of his thumb, that he was going to the Shangri-la.

They moved off toward the higher density of the Strip. Along its edges, flat-topped stucco dives with frenetic neon signs advertised free breakfasts, ninety-nine-cent baseball caps, single-deck blackjack, and other lures for the tattooed set.

At a stoplight, Lasky watched a couple, quarreling, by the looks of it, stumble drunk out of a place called Ned's. The man wore a purple undershirt and jeans. The woman was stuffed into ill-fitting shorts with pasty clumps of flesh oozing out along the edges. The couple was blinded by the heat and glare of the day, but only momentarily. "You hadda double down, didn't you?" the woman screamed, loud enough so Lasky could hear it inside the air-conditioned cab.

When Lasky was a very young man, he enjoyed dog-ass bars like that one, believing the hard-living outcasts inside were astute adventurers.

"Hey," the driver said, pulling away as the light turned, "I know some dynamite girls, you interested?" Lasky looked into the rearview mirror set above the carpeted dashboard and saw one eyebrow across two deep-set dark eyes. After a full minute without answer, the driver said, "What you want, man?"

"I just want a ride to the Shangri-la," Lasky said. "And that's all I want. Don't hustle me."

"Hey, I was trying to make you happy, man. Thas all. Like it's hard to know what's right sometimes, you know? Some a these *madre-chingas*, like they gonna write you up, they think you not friendly, you know? So like I try to keep my ass covered, thas all. Nothing personal, man. Is nothing against you, you know? Life is hard, man."

The driver said all this without turning around, something Lasky appreciated. He like the ones who watched the road. They were on a wide avenue now that cut through a Leave-it-to-Beaver development of moderately priced houses and well-mowed lawns. "Okay, pal. Nothing personal," Lasky told him. "I just had a bad night."

The driver's self-righteous frown immediately turned to a smile in the rearview mirror. Gold tooth. "Dint we all, man? I ain't had a good night since I hit eleven thou in keno, and that was like, I don't know, couple years, anyways. I don't know you or nothing, but I tell you, it pisses me off that I own this cab and still I got to watch out for my license all the time. You shoulda seen what I had to do to get it. They tell you go there, you go there, and they say, no man, you come here second. Go back to the first place again. Know what I mean? They had me running around like . . .like I was in hell, man."

"You've got a good deal here," Lasky said. "You've got your own business, the sun is shining. Things could be a lot worse. Lots of people out there would trade with you. Most people."

"Thas what everybody tell me, man."

"Where did you hit the keno?" Lasky said. A weary question, a reflex. Let the conversation sink to the dumbest available level.

"You shoulda seen it, man. I'm in the Sahara, and I'm down to like nothing. They beat me down in blackjack and that damn wheel a fortune? So I put two bucks on all my kids' birthdays? Six spots. I just had time to get the bet down. Nother minute, I woulda missed it, had to kill myself, right? You shoulda seen me. Like I went crazy, man. I look at those numbers like lit up on the wall, you know? Coont believe it."

"And that's how you bought your cab?"

"Thas right. Usually when I play my kids' birthdays, I play at least five bucks, maybe ten sometimes, you know? This time, like I was all pissed off, you know, so I only played the deuce. Ten bucks woulda paid me like sixty thou. But like what're you gonna do, right?"

Someday, Lasky thought, someone will tell a tale of a gambling victory not tinged with regret.

They pulled up to the Shangri-la, one of the older original joints along the Strip. It seemed almost like a dwarf next to the newer theme park casinos around it—the vast new networks of guest rooms, children's attractions, and shopping arcade come-ons arranged around the gambling tables that broke and battered their guests before tossing them back on the Strip like crumpled coin wrappers.

A snappy doorman who must have been poaching inside his polyester suit opened the rear door, and a rush of heat entered the cab. "You still play those numbers?" Lasky asked the driver.

"All the time, man. I hit 'em again. You see."

❀

Two superwelterweights in sweatshirts sparred, workman-like, in a ring set up inside one of the ballrooms. A trainer shouted instructions to the younger one, a light-brown black kid with a tireless piston of a jab. His sparring partner danced side to side without much success, taking punches. Only a few spectators were sprinkled around the straight-backed padded chairs that were set in rows around the ring. Making his way down a fat red carpet, Lasky found Max the Grind seated with Joe the Dentist at a large round table off in a corner. The tablecloth was spotted from some dinner event the night before. Grinder was just finishing a peach.

"This kid's fighting in three weeks," Grinder told Lasky, keeping his eyes on the ring. "You should watch for it. I hear Bitsy owns a piece of him." He turned to face Lasky. "You know, you really ought to use a little diplomacy with this guy Stalisi. Schmucks like him, they get very touchy when you smudge their wingtips. It's easier to just feed their delusions a little."

"Really?" Lasky said. "When's the last time you fed delusions to anybody?"

"Last time I got laid."

Grinder reminded Lasky of a very bright FBI agent he used to work with when he was stuck prosecuting inter-state car thieves. Rather than accept a transfer, the agent quit. He liked it here. Lasky heard he was doing well producing and selling instructional videos on home security.

"You learn anything about those dead guys?" Lasky said.

"Yeah, we know a little. The kid seems to have been an innocent bystander, and the other one was a very bad boy, mostly a meth dealer. And he wanted to talk to you. Fact is, he did talk to you."

"You really think I heard anything?" Lasky answered. "I'd have told you last night if you'd asked me."

"We did ask you," Grinder said.

"No, your goombah did."

"Can't blame him for asking," the Dentist said. "Sees a mouse and he figures it'll squeal for a little cheese."

"What did you want to see me about, Grinder?" Lasky said, ignoring the Dentist.

"What a you think? We need that cargo, Terrance."

"Then you should have stopped Doctor Endomorph here from shooting all those holes into your suspect."

The Dentist started to reply, but Grinder interrupted. "The guy had a sawed-off. I'm not going to second-guess Joe on that. But now we need that cargo back."

"I'm not stupid enough to try to rip your people off," Lasky said.

"They're not my people," Grinder replied. "I'm just try-ing to solve a crime."

"Sure," Lasky said. "Look, I didn't hear what Berkeley whispered. But the only way to prove it is to let myself get tortured to death."

"Nice idea, mouse," the Dentist said. He turned to Grinder. "Mouse isn't so dumb after all."

"How much did they really take?" Lasky asked Grinder.

"A lot more than you could ever use, Terrance. Hey, I know that shithead biker told you where the loot was. You tell me now, no arguments, no haggling, you get forty K. Otherwise this thing could get very nasty."

"Forty thousand to get back eighteen thousand," Lasky said. "Interesting numbers. Look, I know you and Tonto here are too sweet to do anything desperate, but if by some chance anything did happen to me, and let's say, just for the sake of argument, I did know anything about the where-abouts of that cargo—"

"Just for the sake of argument," Grinder said.

"Well," Lasky said, "an hour later, it could be every-where you don't want it to be. And then it won't matter what I say, will it?"

Joe the Dentist let out a deep sigh of disgust. Grinder, fin-ished with his peach, lit a cigarette. A clean man who smelled like scorched earth nonetheless. "You got Tangeli covering for you?"

Lasky didn't answer.

"You figure you can sit back and get a better price. You're smarter than that, Terrance. This isn't like you." Grinder threw the smoking match on the dirty tablecloth. "Stakes are too high. Just deal yourself out. You can shoot a lot of craps with forty thousand."

"Speaking of which, you owe me eight hundred and fifty dollars," Lasky said.

"How do you figure?" Grinder said.

"I had four fives against three good hands when you and your friend busted up the game. You owe me at least eight fifty. You can take it out of those bills you borrowed off Berkeley."

The Dentist spoke up. "You never had eight hundred and

fifty bucks in your life. That gook whore a yours couldn't earn it in a lifetime."

"My my, the old good cop-bad cop routine," Lasky said. "You guys been watching reruns again?"

Without changing expression, Joe the Dentist reached over and grabbed Lasky's shoulder in a huge fist. It seemed almost businesslike. A frog scooping up a fly. But then the Dentist spoke again, squeezing harder. "Listen, mouse. You want on the payroll? Then you don't pull this shit."

Lasky felt his shoulder might snap like a chicken bone.

Grinder played peacemaker. "Fellas—"

Lasky reached with his free hand into the small of his back and came up with a pistol he stuck in the Dentist's snout. He could feel the bristles of the Old Testament beard against his gun hand. Out of the corner of his eye, he saw the prizefighters dive for cover.

"What do you think, Grinder?" Lasky said. "Isn't it time you traded in your gorilla?" Lasky tried to sound matter-of-fact through the pain in his shoulder. The Dentist neither increased nor relaxed the pressure.

"Terrance," Grinder addressed him, "take it easy, okay? We're all on the same side."

Lasky addressed Joe the Dentist, who appeared unruffled. "See, dummy, Grinder doesn't want me dead just now. Right Grinder? So even if you managed to get the drop on me, he'd most likely shoot you himself. Wanna see?"

"You made your point, Terrance," Max the Grind said. "Now put it down, will you?"

"I just pulled a gun on a cop," Lasky said. "You should have me arrested, don't you think? Take me downtown to see some real cops."

"I get it," Grinder said. "So take it easy."

Lasky eased the barrel off the Dentist's face but still

pointed it at him. The Dentist sneered and let go of his shoulder. Lasky resisted the urgency to touch it, massage the agony. The prizefighters rose warily.

"Being on the take gets complicated sometimes, doesn't it?" Lasky said. "You owe me eight fifty out of your little fund," he told Grinder. He lowered the gun some more and held out his left hand, palm open.

"You're a lawyer!" Grinder said. "What kind of lawyer packs a piece, for Christ's sake? You could be disbarred."

"Start proceedings," Lasky said.

"Three hundred," Grinder said finally.

"Eight," Lasky replied.

Three Shangri-la security guards burst through the far door, guns drawn. The fighters dropped to the canvas again as Lasky froze, fearful of being shot by a nincompoop. Grinder quieted the guards down in short order, and they exited with chests out and stomachs in, as cops do after standing up to trouble. The prizefighters and trainer followed them out the door.

Eventually Grinder turned over five fifty. Then he asked the Dentist to take a walk. The big man started toward the door, then turned. "You're just a snitch now," he told Lasky. "Just another fucking snitch. We got hundreds like you, sheenie."

Sheenie. There it was. Lasky could react, in which case he'd hear it again, or he could ignore it. In which case he'd hear it again. "I've always loved America, but it's never loved me back," Lasky's father once told him. His father claimed he could tell anti-Semites just from the inflection in their voices. Some name would come up in conversation, and Lasky's father would inject, "Jew-hater." Errol Flynn. "Jew-hater." John Wayne. "Jew-hater."

"How do you know?" asked Lasky's mother, a sweet exasperated Wasp not privy to the broad reach of anti-Semitism.

"By the voice," his father would answer. Or sometimes, "Just by his attitude." Or maybe, "Just look at him."

"Were they talking about Jews?" mom would ask him.

"Doesn't matter. They can be talking about geometry, and if they don't like Jews, I can tell." Then he laughed to show that maybe he was kidding. Or maybe he wasn't.

When the Dentist was gone, Lasky massaged his shoulder at last. "Why'd you have to pull his chain like that?" Grinder said. "You know they don't call him the Dentist cause he's nice to everybody's teeth."

"But sometimes it's helpful, having a looney partner," Lasky said.

"Cuts both ways," Grinder said. "But he's my partner."

"Your loyalty is touching," Lasky said.

"You're still a smart ass," Grinder said. "But I'd like to see you come out ahead on this."

Lasky rose and gave a mock salute.

"What about the cargo?" Grinder said.

"I'll poke around, see what I can find out."

"Work this fast," Grinder said.

# CHAPTER FIVE

# Eye-in-the-Sky

Lasky shoved two more green chips onto the Pass Line as the stickman shouted "Coming out! New Shooter, new shooter!" The stickman's voice had a sorrowful tone salted with gravel and toughness, as though he were doing a long stretch in maximum security. His gnarled face was fused into the telltale Vegas scowl, that distinct deadpan expression which told Lasky or anyone else who cared to look that he had seen it all and that there was nothing left to enthuse him except perhaps very large sums of money, which, quite correctly, he did not expect to obtain.

This new shooter he advertised—a cadaverous man at the far end of the crap table—actually wasn't new at all. The dice were merely coming back to him once more after circling all the players in round after round of heartache. As Lasky saw the thin hairy arm with the long tattoo reach for the dice, he said, "Christ, it's him again," and took back one of the two green chips.

"No, I think this was the guy, he didn't do so bad a couple turns ago," the player next to Lasky said.

Lasky wasn't sure now. The previous dice rolls were already blurring like a hopscotch layout in a drizzle. "Well, it's what he does now that counts," Lasky said, wishing he'd taken Grinder's hundred and fifty and left instead of hanging around to fall into yet another uphill battle to get even.

The cavernous Shangri-la could still attract a fair-sized crowd. But it was your basic ill-defined gambling hall topped by a generic stack of guest rooms, and therefore fighting an uphill battle against the huge new theme-park joints whose carpets weren't yet polluted by ashes or tears and whose cherub employees were so diligent they practically squeaked.

The Shangri-la's main claim to fame these days was its crew of cocktail waitresses. They weren't dressed in togas or medieval tutus, but they were all prettier than waitresses had a right to be—scantily clad, tawny young women from places like Utah and Georgia, with fresh shampoos, tight bellies, and sweet, larcenous smiles. Management got rid of them at approximately age thirty-two, depending on genetics and how much time they spent pedaling stationary bicycles.

A brunette vocalist in satin sang Cole Porter along the side of the action. Her phrasing was achingly perfect, and she was backed up by a tight pop quintet which really cared. But no one paid any attention.

❧

"If he's got the cargo," Stalisi said, "why the hell is he playing for peanuts right under our noses? Who's he trying to kid?"

Stalisi watched the top of Lasky's head on a bank of TV screens with Bitsy Rossman and the crew from the eye-in-the-sky room above the gaming area. The shooter threw the dice past Lasky.

"You hang around here long enough," Bitsy said, "it wouldn't surprise you. We see customers worth millions sweating over a few bucks. We see guys worth nothing at all who'll get on a roll and try to raise the stakes all the way to heaven."

"This guy looks like a fucking dummy to me," Stalisi said.

"He's a fuckup, sure," the old man said. "But I wouldn't be so quick to call him a dummy. Grinder says he went to law school at . . . where was it? Princeton, Yale, one a those. He was on Wall Street, for Christ's sake."

"I thought he was with the Feds," Stalisi replied without emotion. Trying not to react. Evidently Bitsy knew Stalisi's law school had been situated above a shopping mall.

The government job came later, Bitsy explained, "After he started fucking up."

Stalisi was feeling his way, not sure how to respond to this gnarly old bastard. Treat the kike like a made guy, Stalisi's uncle had said. Only his uncle never referred to Bitsy as a kike. "Use your manners," his uncle said, "but don't kiss his ass, neither." Whatever the hell that meant. He was supposed to walk some kind of fine line. But he wasn't much good at fine lines. Didn't know how to categorize this stringy dinosaur everyone had to look up when they needed something done in Vegas.

At first, Stalisi wasn't even sure how to address him. "Bitsy" sounded too much like a girl's name. So Stalisi refrained from calling him anything at all. A poor compromise. It made his conversation too impersonal, almost impudent. And how could he be impudent to somebody employed by his family?

Finally, when Stalisi asked him about the new competition down the street, the old man replied, "There's an ebb and flow to these things, Louis. Do your friends call you Lou?"

"Yeah, Lou," Stalisi said. So now they were Lou and Bitsy.

"These new joints," Bitsy said, "we don't own a piece, but they buy our booze, our furniture, they sign contracts with our union people. We're doing okay. And they're not such an improvement over our joints. Some of this new stuff they got, it's downright stupid.

"Over at the Treasure Island? Before they opened, they spent six months building this computerized bar. Bartender's supposed to press buttons on the hose and call up any drinks he wants. First night, he presses Beefeater, out comes VO. He hits the J&B button, he gets a shpritz of Gordon's vodka. They got thousands of new customers lined up at the bar, and the bartenders are taking odds every time they try to mix a drink."

As Bitsy laughed at his own story, Stalisi had the distinct feeling he was laughing not at Treasure Island but at Stalisi.

"You know, Lou," Bitsy said, "it's right to worry about some things but not about things you can't control. And you especially shouldn't worry about things that don't exist at all except in your worries."

Fucking kike.

Stalisi wondered if the old fart had a deal with Lasky. Lasky could be a Jew name. Jew or Polack. Stalisi would find out. Wouldn't be the first time Jews worked out something like this among themselves.

Stalisi pulled a small, leather-bound memo book and an

attached gold pen and quickly scribbled "Lasky—Jew?" on a single page.

"You never get a short count from Bitsy," his uncle had said. "You can tell time by the guy." But now it looked like these new joints were about to eat the outfit's lunch, and if the cash didn't turn up from this heist, Stalisi wouldn't write any policies on the sheenie's ass.

Meanwhile, Bitsy Rossman didn't look disturbed at all. Acted like he was having a hot day at the track. Feet up on a chair, bullshitting with the crew and managing to make everybody comfortable but Stalisi.

❧

A dapper, fidgety player across from Lasky suddenly turned to him. "You feel it?" he said.

"Excuse me?" Lasky said, not sure he understood. "What'd you say?"

The dapper player smiled, then backing up and bobbing his head like a prizefighter, looked toward the other end of the table as though he spotted his favorite paramour off in the distance. What he watched was the cadaverous shooter with the tatooed arms, sunken yellow cheeks, discount toupee, and saggy brown trousers.

The dapper player wore an Armani jacket and an emerald earring that sparkled like an electric wind chime. His pointy features could have been assembled by a cartoonist for the *New Yorker*. One of the Shangri-la's treasured few high rollers, he played behind a stack of purple five-hundred-dollar chips, fingering and rubbing them like worry beads. The dapper player was a fount of tics and grimaces, snorts and winks and twitches. Watching him, Lasky wondered how he played for such stakes without immolating himself through spontaneous combustion.

The cadaverous shooter rolled a six. The dapper player, fumbling and wide-eyed, placed four white chips behind his two chips on the Pass Line, taking odds the shooter would roll another six before he rolled a seven. Lasky also took the odds, with two green twenty-five-dollar chips. The shooter rolled.

"Six!" the stickman yelled. "Back-to-back. Hard six! Pay the line." Players clapped their hands, cheered, laughed as the dice crew poured payoffs around the table. Because they desperately craved a winning table, some of the players acted like they were at a winning table, blocking out memories of all the miserable rolls they'd suffered here previously.

The next roll: "Eleven, pay the line!" yelled the stickman. The dice crew, still methodical, paid off again, slapping more chips around the table as new wagers fell like raindrops and the sweet smell of a hot table floated out beyond the betting circle.

Instant converts buzzed around the action, snatching up remaining spots. Lasky saw a couple of old guys desert their wives and scramble over from the showroom line, where supplicants without any juice waited like pathetic sheep for leftover tables.

The craps players, less like strangers now, were forming a mob of souls in tune, anonymous *companeros* who aimed to levitate attitude into reality as the dice came back to the thin, cadaverous man. His expression, as before, revealed no messages.

"Don't change a thing," murmured Lasky, snapping down chips on the Pass Line. The shooter rolled two more naturals. Each time table spirits leaped higher. The next come-out roll was a nine. If the shooter could repeat it, the Pass Line would once again pay even money, plus an additional 3-to-2 win for wagers behind the line, where the players threw most of their action.

Anything was okay now except seven, the one number that would bring it all down. The cadaverous shooter proceeded to roll a magnificent series of twos and threes and sixes and eights and fives, elevens, and lots and lots of tens and fours—each tumble providing the players a harvest of chips on their side bets against the house. They won on numbers and Come bets and the rest of the crazy selection of mathematical propositions spread around the table.

Winning and the expectation of more winning transformed the players into a cabal of hopped-up savages, a cargo cult greeting a succulent shipment as they belted out demands to the sweating crew. "Press the eight!" "All the hard ways!" "Buy the number!" As though their decisions were layered with intelligence.

Every roll sated the alchemy of the mob, then raised it another notch. There was no more room along the rail. The table was a closed club, a submarine already sailed, torpedoing the shit out of enemy tubs which were left a smoking, shrieking, sinking flotsam of defeat. The cadaverous player, who was the cause, the fountain, the magic source of victory—his arm cranking out like a benevolent crane—had somehow tamed the possibilities. Number after number. Cheer after cheer.

But then Lasky heard a scream of undisguised agony pierce the joy. "Don't touch that!" It was the player next to him, who, like so many crapshooters, looked old enough to have learned the game on a World War II troop ship. He also looked ready to bite the waitress in half.

"But it's empty," she protested weakly, holding up his highball glass.

"Oh, Jesus, don't touch it, put it back, put it back," he yelled.

"Is that your lucky glass?" another player said. "Oh no, it's his lucky glass, goddammit! You trying to queer the dice?"

She returned the glass to the holder along the rail. The shooter rolled the nine. "Pay the line!" yelled the stickman.

The owner of the glass flipped the waitress a five-dollar chip. "Touch it again, sweetheart," he commanded. "But don't take it away."

There is no time on a winning crap table. The start of a great roll is difficult to see, floating in the mist that hangs over the ebb and flow of choppy dice. But all over Vegas, there were thousands of crap shooters who watched for its signs. They were rooted like trees or moving from casino to casino. They watched and waited and grew old or melancholy or bitter, trying to believe they would find the right place at the right time and know what to do. And except for Lasky and the other players around him, they were all at the wrong tables.

At this table, the players pounded each other like Super Bowl victors. They toasted fortune, barked, spit, jumped, giggled. All their vague, dispiriting worries were gone. They had no broken dreams, no families, no responsibilities, no ailments. And they so loaded the table with new wagers that the blue felt layout was barely discernible underneath.

Because the players had earned their stakes with blocks of time that were life itself, the winning table extended that life. "Now we got 'em, now we got 'em," somebody screamed.

Lasky, caught up in the mystic swell, was dimly aware that across the way, the dapper, fidgety player was shoving stack after stack on the Pass Line. The pit boss grabbed a phone and barked for help from a superior. The rest of the dice crew tried to look disappointed for the bosses as they lapped up frenzied showers of tips.

"I believe!" Lasky shouted, and he shoved a small multi-colored mountain into harm's way. The pit boss was off the phone now, no doubt crossing his toes to jinx the son-ofabitch with the dice. The stickman shoved over five dice, the cadaverous shooter selected two, and tossed them, his face still blank.

"I waited all my life to find this table," Bitsy said, watching the monitor. "And what happens? I'm on the wrong side of the action."

The cadaverous shooter rolled a four. "A tough point," said the player next to Lasky, pulling his bets off the numbers. But most players tossed even more bets onto the layout. Lasky, ahead by a couple thousand, let it ride. "One more," he said.

Another long series of numbers followed. Each roll earned some players chips but did not affect the bigger action along the Pass Line and just behind it on the odds. Only another four or the dreaded seven could settle these bets. The dapper player was strangely quiet and untwitching as Lasky felt waves of terror and pleasure roll over the table like passing storms and sunbreaks.

Then the cadaver threw the two and two. "Four! Hard

four! Pay the line!" Delirium. Players shrieked and babbled like toddlers as the grim-faced dice crew swiftly paid off the towering stacks of wagers, using a new cart of chips brought alongside for the occasion.

Lasky shoved most of his stack back on the Pass Line and pressed his bets on the numbers, letting them all ride. "One more," he said.

He looked over toward the dapper player's spot along the rail and couldn't find him. Casino functionaries were methodically collating his mountain of chips, cashing him in. Here and there, other players had slipped away like deserters, their places taken by eager new recruits. Lasky counted his own chips on the Pass Line—fifty three hundred, fifty four hundred—

The cadaverous player came out with an eight. More merriment, more bets.

Fifty five hundred, fifty six hundred—

"Seven out!"

The stickman announced it like any other roll, as though nothing of consequence had occurred. Lasky and the other diehards, alone and betrayed, applauded the great run by the cadaverous man. But now they would have to start all over again. "Coming out!" yelled the stickman. "New shooter."

"You been inside the MGM this year?" Turnquist said. "It's even better now. It's amazing."

"No, but I've heard about it," Bags said politely.

"Really, it's amazing. I wouldn't mind kicking back there for a weekend with the family. The kids would go nuts."

The wizard of Oz, Dorothy, balloons, rides, pirates, arcade games, and roller coasters. The giant new casinos were a mosaic that mixed gamblers and children in an unsorted orgy of pleasures that would no doubt breed new, bigger generations of suckers when the children grew up. Yet Bags knew that no matter how transparent the marketing strategies, he was still powerless against them. He was like a chain-smoking physician.

The waitress brought agent Turnquist his soup and spinach salad and agent Hernandez his French dip with fries and Bags more coffee. Raymond Chandler's cops would never order soup and spinach salad. It's what the world had come to. Stairmaster cops.

They were in the same old booth in the same old Denny's on Charleston Avenue. They'd already discussed the menu, Turnquist's cholesterol count, Hernandez's boat, and two or three minutes of current events. Any minute now Turnquist would zero in on what he wanted from Bags and Hernandez would threaten Bags a little and then Bags could finish drinking coffee and get the hell out.

"You know, if you'd just show some gainful employment," Hernandez said, "it would sure help us keep that parole officer off you." Hernandez, as far as Bags or anyone else could determine, had no Latin blood whatsoever. He was an excitable, round-faced little man, and somewhat dimwitted, which in his case made him more cruel.

"Counting cards is strictly legal," Bags said. "You know that."

"In a way it is," Hernandez said. "But it's not a job, either."

They all knew Bags' fat-ass parole officer wouldn't even know his name if it weren't for these two. But he couldn't dare allude to the truth of the matter. That's how powerless he was against them. All this because in a moment of weakness, he'd borrowed a few thousand from a little foundation grant to cover some commodity shorts. Later, he'd had fourteen months in stir to think about it—about the unscheduled audit, the congressional hypocrites hungry for airtime and Ivy League blood. Cockroaches had better luck than he did.

Sometimes he feared this Hernandez, just for laughs, really intended to make him take a job in a convenience store somewhere. When he felt low, he could come in and order up a Slim Jim and a Slurpee from the former Yale professor.

"You staying away from those other games?" Hernandez asked him.

"Pretty much," Bags said.

"Pretty much. Pretty much isn't how you told us it's going to be."

"I appreciate your concern," Bags said.

"See? He appreciates us," Hernandez said. "You do appreciate us, don't you, Professor?"

"Bags is doing okay," Turnquist said. "Bags has nine lives and ninety-nine careers ahead of him." He gave Hernandez a quick, impatient look and turned the discussion to business. Once again, Bags was grateful that FBI Agent Turnquist and T-man Hernandez genuinely disliked each other.

Bags had learned in the joint that federal strike forces, despite their inspring publicity releases and gritty nomenclatures, were staffed by each contributing agency's least productive agents. Supervisors always saved their best people for their own cases and threw the task forces oddballs and rejects from the bottom of the roster. Turnquist and Hernandez were each living reminders to the other of his own second-rate status.

Not surprisingly, they wanted something on the shooting

last night, which they knew, of course, was tied in with the hijacking.

"What did the Vegas cops tell you about it?" Bags said. "They were there."

Turnquist smiled. "I think we'll ask the questions if you don't mind."

"If I had more to go on, it might help me find something out."

"That may be true," Turnquist said. He took an envelope out of his breast pocket and slipped out a small, somewhat blurred photograph of an insolent, handsome man who paid a lot of attention to his hair. "Did you see this guy last night?"

"He was there," Bags said. They didn't seem surprised.

"You know who he is?"

"He came in with those city detectives."

"Yeah, but do you know who he is?"

"No."

"Find out, okay? And then call right away."

Bags wouldn't inquire why they didn't just ask Grinder or his Dentist sidekick. It was no secret that the Feds weren't on good terms with the local cops.

He would call Turnquist in a day or two and give him Stalisi's name. He was almost certain they were just playing games with him, that they already knew it. Stalisi had probably been spotted by their airport watch. It looked like an airport kind of picture. Stalisi wasn't the type to drive here across country like a slot player.

❦

Lasky, helping out behind the bar, plunged batches of dirty glasses into the sink, occasionally looking out at the solitary patrons who'd rather sit in this smoky refuge than face whatever was home. It was after dinner, and Bob's was filling up. Finally Snapper approached, ignoring the stares that had followed her all her life. Even back in Malaysia, her tall, succulent beauty must have been unique. Here in the grainy Nevada desert, it was melting, other-worldly.

Lasky wiped his hands quickly, then dug into his pocket. "Hi kid, I've got sixty bucks here for you."

Without any expression, she took the bills. "No stories to tell?"

"The usual. I was dealt four fives in a game of stud and they ended up on the floor with two corpses."

"I heard that one," she said. "How have you been otherwise?"

"I think there might be a curse on me," he said. He told her about the beggar outside the Mirage. He was no ordinary beggar, Lasky said. He looked strong and confident, like he was on a mission or something. And how did he get there? Ordinarily, the cops kept beggars off the Strip. "It seemed like he was waiting for me," he concluded.

"You believe that a little, don't you?" she said.

"Just a little," he confided.

"Maybe it wasn't a curse. Maybe he saw it was time to change your luck," she said.

"But I'd just won two hundred bucks."

"That's not what I mean," she said.

"Are you getting metaphysical again?" he said. When a beggar approached, you had two seconds to pronounce judgment—con man, psychopath, or deserving soul. They asked too much of you. Lasky should try to explain this, but he was nervous talking with her, as he still was once in awhile. Her unblinking, unfeigned confidence could still overwhelm him.

Snapper studied him, then exhaled a cloud of cigarette smoke. "Lasky," she said, "just how much does money mean to you anyway?"

"See? You are getting metaphysical again."

"Because you're taking some real risks here. And I don't know why. Do you?"

She'd been waiting to confront him; he knew she would, and still he wasn't ready. Even when she was upset with him, Snapper's voice was sweet. No doubt attached to her vulva by silken threads. In a fraction he was aroused. It was heaven to sleep with someone who could still do that to you.

"You mean why do I gamble?" he said.

"Yes."

"Probably the same reason everybody does, kid. To get it over with." He plunged his hands back into the soapy water.

A fat man approached Snapper from behind and placed his hand on her rear. He whispered in her ear and tried to escort her away. Some hick who thought you could just grab her off the shelf like a six-pack. Snapper stared at him a split second then turned away in disdain.

"Brilliant," she told Lasky. "But what are you going to do about those stolen bills?"

"Stolen bills?"

"The hijacked money, Lasky. The money everyone is talking about. They're going to kill you for it. You know that, don't you?"

"Let's talk about this another time, okay?"

The fat man, just drunk enough, tried to pull her away again. She turned and smacked him on the ear. "Get away from me, you sonofabitch," she said. He stepped back, wide-eyed, as though squirted by an orchid. Lasky was bewildered, too. Never before had he seen Snapper even raise her voice. She never had to.

Ignoring the new stares from customers up and down the bar, she told Lasky. "You're too special to go along? I'm telling you, they're going to kill you. Believe it."

"Maybe," he said, feeling stupid.

"There is no maybe, Lasky. They're going to kill you if you don't go along."

"If I don't lie back and enjoy it," he said. He was already sorry a half-second before the words tumbled out of his mouth. She walked off without another word.

Lasky shouted after her, "I didn't mean that." Then softer, to himself, "I didn't mean that."

# CHAPTER SIX

# A Vast Prison Yard

Bob Tangeli wrapped up an M-1 carbine and two banana clips for a stout, middle-aged couple in bowling shirts. "You decide you want that trigger adjusted, just bring it back," he told them. He enjoyed arming citizens.

As they exited with their purchase, a second couple brushed past them at the door. They both had delicate, Waspy features. She wore boy-style blonde hair and wire-rimmed glasses. Also finely tuned jeans, simple jewelry, and just the right blouse showing just the right cleavage to announce herself with well-planned understatement. She had a face Tangeli had seen many times, but never in person. She was Lasky's ex-wife.

The guy with her wore the sort of fuzzy shoes and lumpy corduroy sport jacket preferred by assistant professors and animal-rights activists. The ex-wife asked Cap for something, but Tangeli couldn't hear her over the reggae.

"I ain't no maitre d'," he heard Cap reply. "I'm a bouncer."

She turned to her companion and laughed, looking genuinely amused. She didn't back off, the way most people do from Cap. Just then three young men entered. One wore a python around his neck. Cap reached out and stopped him. "Hey, no reptiles."

"Reptiles eat rodents, man," the snake man protested.

"We take care of our own rodents," Cap told him.

The attractive couple tried to maintain some distance from the snake. Its head moved lazily around like a radar scanner protruding from the neck of its owner as the tongue, machinelike, busily searched for something interesting.

Tangeli, himself no lover of snakes, kept one hand on his nine-millimeter Browning and stayed well behind the counter. Meanwhile, Bags, who'd been sitting at the bar, approached the couple like he'd been watching for them. The ex-wife kissed him on both cheeks, European style, and the guy gave him a suburban handshake. Bags led them toward a table somewhere, the kid in the corduroy coat gliding past the snake like he was moving along a twelfth-floor ledge.

Tangeli heard Cap say, "No arguments, understand? I hate snakes."

"Don't tell me you're afraid of Al. Here, pet 'em. Go on, Al. Say hi to the man."

There was a scream of fright and disgust.

Snapper, reading her dog-eared copy of Camus's *The Stranger*, lit a cigarette and looked up to see Bags wander past her booth with a couple of Mother Jones tourists. She caught Bags's eye and asked them all to sit down. "Great,"

he mumbled, along with some other words Snapper couldn't make out.

When Bags made his introductions, Snapper didn't pay attention to their names, but the blonde seemed somehow familiar. She was pushing forty, maybe beyond that, but very well preserved, with a proud, expressive face that belonged in a Bergman film.

"Well, what are you working on these days, Dr. McBannister?" the young man asked Bags. A sexy young man who clearly knew all about Bags's downfall.

"A little of this and a little of that," Bags said.

"It's not an easy time for most people in this economy," the blonde said. As she spoke, she reached over and caressed Bags's arm, acting as though she'd known him all his life. Somehow she made it work. She was a tidy package.

Lasky! That was the name! Terry's ex-wife!

"We could use some ideas for the economy around Madison," the young man, a puppy on Mayor Laura Lasky's staff said. And he went on to tell them more than Snapper cared to know about the financial tribulations of city governance in Madison, Wisconsin—ancient tax codes, hidebound special interests, and the like.

Meanwhile, the ex-wife glanced toward Snapper, then away, then back again. Snapper understood. She held attention like a glass eye. Was she Chinese? Mexican? Some kind of Hawaiian hybrid? The eyes were not quite oriental, the soft accent not quite discernible. Too tall for a Filipino. Liberal types like these two always seemed to be the most racially obsessed. It was also clear the ex-wife suspected she was a working girl.

Were Snapper short and homely, everyone would be less curious about her origins and line of work. Most Americans—when they discovered she was from Malaysia—behaved as though that cleared everything up. They weren't quite sure just where Malaysia was, but it was an exotic, mysterious concept—an Alexandria or a Jupiter. They assumed people from such a place ought to look puzzling.

They didn't realize Malaysia was not an answer, but just the start of another puzzle—a land of three tangled races whose souls remained apart. In Malaysia, race was so scalding an issue it could not even be discussed legally except within certain limited and well-defined parameters. So no matter how curious people became, no one could dare ask the precise question: What are you?

"May I ask? What are you?" a woman at a nearby table called over sweetly. "I mean where are you from? We were trying to figure it out." Snapper gave her a look that would freeze hell.

"She's a Sagittarius from South Philly," answered sweet Bags. The woman and her two male companions were obvious Plasticine worshipers from Pastor Pinky's Temple of Worth—sweet and red-cheeked as Olympic skaters. Like all of Pinky's goofballs, they were dressed for success. After an uncomfortable silence, the tactlessness of the intrusion became apparent even to them. They mumbled too many apologies, then paid their check and cleared out faster than dignity allowed.

"Pinks," Bags explained to the Madison pair. "They're a . . . sort of a cult."

"A cable cult," Snapper injected, "as in cable TV."

"Their leader comes in here," Bags said. "He calls himself a pastor now. Pastor Pinky. He's got a slimy little show that he syndicates to a few hayseed stations."

"Pinky was a writer once," Snapper said. "A biographer.

I'm sure you've heard of him. P. Eric Dillingham. He's been written about here and there. Like you," she smiled.

"Not lately," the ex-wife said. True enough. The media were bored to death with leftover radicals and their causes. Abbie Hoffman had to kill himself to win back fifteen minutes of attention. In a few years, if this lioness of Cambodia didn't change her luck, she could become another figure of fun—in media hell with Jane Fonda and the rest.

"P. Eric Dillingham," Roy Fetherling, the earnest puppy said. "Now I remember him. Pop biographer of some kind. Funny how the world turns."

"It wasn't so much the world turning," Bags said, "as a snake shedding skin."

Personally, Snapper found Pinky's much-discussed, heavily footnoted biography of John Lennon mildly amusing. As the author P. Eric Dillingham, Pinky had concluded that Lennon was no poet of peace but rather a brute tortured by homosexual longings.

"You must understand, he created an inner sanctum that was impenetrable during his lifetime. But the facts were there. One just had to piece them together." That was Pinky's key talk-show statement. First to describe Elvis. Later others, including Brian Jones of the Rolling Stones and ultimately Lennon.

In those days Pinky, a Kentucky go-getter who had little use for music of any kind, wore a putative academic persona, giving his utterances on rock 'n' roll a backwoods-meets-ivy halls twist. One by one, as yet another pop-chart giant was felled by drugs or plane crashes or, as in Lennon's case, a crazed fan—author Pinky waded in with his standard 800-page treatment derived from secret sources around the globe.

A star's innumerable wives, mistresses, or trysts were all

pitiful masks of denial. To Pinky, the more they lusted for women, the more queer these guys had to be. And, of course, they were dead as well. For queer or straight, the dead cannot sue.

About the same time book buyers tired of the Dillingham homo-formula, an ex-wife and her lawyers chopped his overleveraged life-style down to a stump. With repo men hot on his trail, he fled to Vegas in a Mercedes, painted it pink, and turned from pop biographies to pop sermons without missing a beat. There was not much admirable about Pinky but much to appreciate. And Snapper had a soft spot for American ingenuity.

Martha, the pregnant waitress, wended through the tables to take their order. Fetherling ordered a beer, but the ex-wife asked for a stinger.

"That might be over our head, but I'll see what I can do," Martha said. She said it kindly, not in her usual brusque fashion. People responded to Laura Lasky. Snapper pictured her in bed with Terry, trying to measure her enthusiasm. She was displeased with the picture.

Excusing herself without explanation, Snapper placed *The Stranger* in her pocketbook and walked off.

"Where *is* she from anyway?" Fetherling said.

"Malaysia," Bags said.

"A Malay. Aren't they Muslims?"

"She was a Malaysian citizen, but not Malay. She's half-Chinese, half-Indian, and definitely not Muslim." Bags didn't like getting drawn into this, as though discussing the offspring of a cocker bred to a Dalmatian.

"Marvelous combination," Fetherling said.

"Quite beautiful," Laura said. "I've never met a Malaysian immigrant before."

"Snapper's an unusual person," Bags said.

"I'll bet she is," Fetherling said. There was a pause for a smirk, but no one actually smirked. They just observed the pause.

"Snapper's an abstract artist," said Bags, who always felt responsible for all awkward silences anywhere in his vicinity. "Quite a good one, really. At least that's what I'm told. That's one of hers over there." He pointed out the large oil painting along the wall. They looked at it briefly, registering neither approval nor disapproval, strangely taciturn on the subject of art.

"She's just a . . .just a friend," Bags added. Foolish thing to say. Just a friend. What could be more important?

In short order, Fetherling and Laura Lasky shifted the conversation back to politics, reciting a standard hate-the-rich theology, excoriating ignorant overpaid executives, assault rifles that sold over the counter like chewing gum, and the lack of free vaccinations for kids. Laura held up her end of the spiel with ease and talent, making Bags always impatient to hear her next sentence even though she'd delivered pretty much the same monologue when he'd first met her at a New York conference. She had sized him up then as a kindred spirit, a common supposition made by liberals thrown together with anyone showing a trace of education and no telltale Republican attire.

He was amazed and terribly flattered to still be on anyone's Rolodex. But somehow she'd tracked him down today and asked to meet. "Why don't you come to my office?" he told her, giving directions to Bob's.

It hurt to remember the days in New Haven when he actually did have an office—and teams of graduate assistants,

subservient as Roman salves, eager as Fetherling. Some of
the females were perhaps as smart and sexy as Laura Lasky.
All of them poring through dull-ass government tomes to
serve him the statistical gems he sprinkled throughout his
books and articles.

That last year, before everything collapsed, he had to
teach only one class in his paradise now lost. The rest of his
time was officially designated for research. There were
even invitations to explain economic hocus-pocus to some
of the smaller TV markets. A network affiliate once dis-
patched a whole camera crew to his office so he could tell
them that silver wouldn't hit six or seven until it could
break out of the five-thirty range. And nobody even snick-
ered. What a wonderful life he had.

But of course when he emerged from Leavenworth—just
when he had something to say—he was cut off from both
mass media and those puerile academic journals no one
read but the people trying to get printed in them. Sometimes he ached to analyze the significance of all the spunky
little mom-and-pop businesses crawling out of the mud of
corporate downsizing. They grew tomatoes, repaired
shoes, ironed shirts, sold weapons, sucked dick. America
was turning into a vast prison yard.

He found himself explaining some of this to Laura Lasky.
He couldn't help it. He wanted her to like him.

After a couple rounds of drinks, she deftly moved the
conversation over to her ex-husband again, as she had on
the phone. She knew they were acquainted. He wondered
what else she knew. "We understand he might be in some
kind of trouble," she said.

Bags answered softly, as though he was bestowing a confidential forecast on a favored investor. "Mrs. Lasky—"

"Laura," she corrected him.

"This is difficult," Bags explained, "because . . . Terry's a friend of mine."

"He's a friend of mine, too," she said.

Bags said, "My guess is that armored car was actually carrying mob money. Around here that usually means money skimmed off the top of the drop."

"The drop?" Fetherling said.

"The total amount of cash and markers that come in on a shift."

"And just how many casinos does the mob skim?" she asked him.

"I wouldn't know. That kind of information is hard to get. Anyway, the word is that . . . Terry, your ex-husband, might know . . . does know, where the money is. That he might be taking delivery. Somehow."

Martha arrived with another tray of drinks, presenting Laura's stinger with a flourish. Lasky stepped up behind her. "When did you start drinking candy?" he asked his ex-wife.

"After you left. It's your replacement," Laura said.

"You look good, kid," he said.

She introduced Lasky to her bookish, boy-faced companion. Bags should have warned Lasky when Fetherling stuck out his hand. Sure enough, he snared the tips of his fingers, squeezing as hard as he could, just as he'd done to Bags earlier.

On third or fourth glance, this Fetherling wasn't as young as Bags first guessed. He was merely one of those people who dressed like a kid and looked younger in glasses, which hid the crow's feet.

"I like your establishment very much," Fetherling told Lasky, who protested that he was just a hired hand.

"You know, creating a bistro is really an art form,"

Fetherling said. He went on to compare saloons to jazz or reggae. "But most of the time the music, the cafe," he said, "it's a series of wrong notes. Like a guitar. Lots of folks can play a guitar, but how many can play it well?"

Bags was sure he'd heard the analogy before, probably in a commentary on one of the publicly owned radio stations. Lasky looked like he had other things on his mind and was in no mood to be dragged into the dull dance of cocktail chatter. "Well, you're right," he said finally. "It's a good joint. But it's just a joint."

He said he had work to do. "See you, kid," he told his ex-wife. He never even inquired what inspired her journey to Las Vegas. Laura Lasky whispered something quick to Fetherling, who then scurried after her ex-husband with a message.

It was an odd little meeting of ex-spouses, but such events are generally awkward under the best of circumstances, and Bags could not even guess what each felt about the other.

# CHAPTER SEVEN

# Drowned-Out Puccini

In Las Vegas, where most surroundings were about as genuine as a golf course, even when Lasky was outside, he usually felt like he was inside. But not here, in the abandoned park. After the city suspended maintenance, the desert reclaimed the site with no trouble at all. Where grass once grew, scrub and sage sprouted from a wasteland of sand packed hard as glass, lending a natural flavor to the place.

The ex-park was suspended halfway between a collection of warehouses and a weary stucco ghetto studded with broken-down fences and crumpled automobiles. At one end, a grid of concrete benches faced a graffiti-encrusted, sun-bleached bandshell where an operatic soprano, a cellist, and a violinist performed for a few dozen mostly elderly spectators scattered among the benches. Lasky sat toward the rear.

The soprano was a prideful middle-aged black woman in a cocktail dress who was probably very close to being the real thing. The relentless neon signs of the Strip threw an ugly pink mist off in the distance, obscuring the night sky and rendering them more alone in the universe.

As the entertainers worked towards the end of an evening of Puccini, they had to compete as always with sounds in the distance—engines, animal yelps, drunken laughter. All of it blended into a kind of low-level backup sludge. But at some point, the brutal squeal of an electronically magnified rap recording began crowding out the other noises.

And after awhile, four hip-hop punks in pirate scarves and ankle-length raincoats rounded a corner fence topped with coiled razor wire and approached the bandshell. One of them carried a Buick-sized ghetto blaster on his shoulder. It was the source of the grinding, assembly-line, barking rap-shout that now competed head-to-head with the classical trio on stage.

The soprano's voice climbed valiantly toward the ecstatic peak of "O Mio Babbino Caro," Puccini's sweet, powerful composition about a girl's love for her father. But as the punks cut across the seats, the ragged bass screech from their boom box drowned her out entirely. The punks loped along like skunks, fearless and slow, and Lasky could see their faces now. They wore the same cruel, bored expressions that were popular in designer-jean ads.

In situations like these, it always seemed to Lasky that everyone else was waiting for him to initiate action, as though he were still the platoon leader. So doing nothing, he felt not just cowardly but disloyal as well. Still, he played the odds, and the odds favored thoughtful cowardice, which he liked to think of as selective bravery. He

would defend his life, but everything else was nego-
tiable.

Even in his younger boisterous days, when Lasky refused to back away from a bar fight, he was careful never
to go outside with an opponent. When he saw harm coming, he stood his ground and punched first. Somebody
would always break up the fight quickly, and he would
never be surprised out in the alley by a weapon, an accomplice, or a tougher man.

It was that same combination of instinct and reasoning
which made him a success in Vietnam, where others
quickly sized him up as someone who had a knack for staying alive. They rarely questioned his judgment and then
only in tentative terms. It made the yoke of leadership even
heavier.

The soprano gave up and waited for the four hip-hop-
pers to pass. As he sometimes did in these situations, Lasky
pretended to himself that he was a certified public accoun-
tant with a busy, long-legged wife on the PTA board in
Boise, Idaho.

Then he spotted Tangeli wheeling toward him. Fortu-
nately, Tangeli was on a different path and did not directly
pass the four punks, who by now were on the way out of
the ex-park. As he reached Lasky, the performers started
up again, as though someone kick-started an operatic juke-
box.

"You know what I was thinking about?" Tangeli said.
"How nice it would be to have my old platoon here . . .open
up on those fuckers with some small arms, maybe a sixty
just for flavor. Bust 'em up low at first to get their attention."

"Real life's never that sweet, is it?" Lasky said. "But hell,
you're the guy from the Woodstock generation, remember?

Love, peace, acid ... That's all those kids need, isn't it? Love and understanding."

"Whaddayou know about it? If you'd a been at Woodstock, it would a turned into World War III."

Tangeli couldn't be more than ten years older than Lasky, but it felt more than that, like a generation at least, as though they had fought two different wars. Tangeli humped trails in the Ia Drang Valley with the First Cav, when everybody was trying to win and GIs weren't yet an embarrassment back home.

By the time Lasky arrived, the grunts of Tangeli's era had already killed off the VC, but the NVA had taken their place, and battlefield outcomes no longer mattered anyway. One of Lasky's scouts said they were all hamsters plucked from an air-conditioned cage Nixon and Kissinger kept in the Pentagon basement.

Tangeli bought two beers from the unofficial vendor, and they settled in, listening to the coiled range of the soprano.

"What ever happened to that other violinist?" Lasky said. "What was his name? Lazar." A thick-chested taciturn man who wrote and published not a bad little book on roulette.

"Went back to Philadelphia," Tangeli said. "Trying to change his luck. Least that's what I heard. Tell me something, willya? I don't mean to pry into your business or anything. But why'd you ever let that woman get away?"

"Laura?" Lasky smiled, remembering. "Lot of reasons. Maybe she didn't want to be married to a poker shill. Maybe I wasn't man enough to be married to a semi-celebrity. Hard to say. If I don't understand myself, how am I gonna understand me and her together? But I'll tell you something about Laura. She's always playing this one note. It's a nice note. Maybe even beautiful. But it's always the same note, and you're never sure if it's real or just artificial. But I'm sure she could say a lot worse about me."

"She's nice, all right," Tangeli said. "Right down to her thighs."

"Well, a lot of guys agreed with you," Lasky said. "She was always at the end of her telephone in two rings. Know what I mean? So efficient, it gave you a hard-on."

"I love that breed."

Lasky thought of his father, who would disagree. His father equated efficiency with sexless drudgery, with the numbing despair of a job. Jobs, he'd once instructed Lasky, were for people too dumb to figure out any other way to make a living.

Someday Lasky ought to tell Bob about his family, about his parents and their consuming desire to always be elsewhere, an elsewhere that was far away. How they periodically dragged Lasky and his little sister to inexplicable little dots on the map they would develop a curiosity about, usually on a far-flung coast somewhere. Tioman Island in the China Sea, Costa Rica's Tamarindo Beach.

But his father never did get out from under a job, not while Lasky knew him. He taught high-school social studies wearing a Rolex he won on an election bet. And he never said goodbye. He left the Rolex behind for Lasky, but eventually his mother sold it for rent and gin.

The soprano was back now at the same point where she had surrendered to the boom box. When she passed it, there was scattered applause. The entertainers finished and took their bows to unusually enthusiastic applause. The soprano began circulating through the ragtag audience with a donation can.

"Did you like opera before you moved to Vegas?" Lasky said.

"Not much," Tangeli said.

"Me neither."

"Your choices start narrowing, you appreciate things," Tangeli said.

"Then why'd you get here late?"

"Don't get around like I used to," Tangeli said. "What'd they offer for the load?"

"Forty K," Lasky said.

"Smart offer. That's Bitsy's way. Enough to make it worth a look, not enough to make him a soft touch. Listen, I've got something I'd like you to handle for me. Pinky's late on his cigarettes again. We can't run a bar without cigarettes. Talk to him willya? He gives me the creeps."

"Okay."

"I meant to ask you—what the hell's your ex-wife doing here, anyway?"

"Angling for some of that money, I expect."

"Figures," Tangeli said. "But it didn't take her long to find out, did it?"

"No, I've been wondering about that myself."

"We're a long way from Wisconsin. Couldn't she just write a letter or something?" Tangeli said.

"I might be dead by the time it's delivered."

"Don't be so sure," Tangeli said. "Bitsy doesn't want anything like that."

"Don't be so sure of that, either."

"It ain't like the old days, Terry. You know that. These mob guys, they rat on each other now just like the other sleazeballs. You get some flunky to whack somebody, the guy gets busted for possession or something, and he'll turn you in for a Valium. Bitsy knows.

"The Chicago guys, they're all used up. Venassio can't order up 200 trigger men with his anchovies anymore. He's got to scrounge—send back to the old country or hire himself bikers or flakey cops. You actually been to Chicago lately? Guineas can't run that town anymore. White people don't even live there. The blacks and Puerto Ricans, they got AR-15s, and they don't scare so easy."

"If the outfit had nothing left," Lasky said, "they wouldn't have been able to skim that money. It takes weight to do that."

Tangeli ticked off the names of three downtown casinos plus the Shangri-la. "I figure that's all they got left," he said. "And yeah, it takes weight. Or maybe just reputation. But these new joints are kicking the old guys' asses. They're finished in this town. It's the fall of the Roman Empire all over again."

"Aren't you exaggerating just a little bit?" Lasky said.

"A little. Maybe even a lot. But I say let them sweat awhile. Look, Terry, you're playing on house money. Don't be so quick to cash in. I ever tell you about the unluckiest night of my life?"

"Constantly," Terry answered.

"The hell I did," Tangeli said. "What it was, I won nine hundred fifty shooting dice. I was dynamite, see? I must a rolled twelve, thirteen passes. Never saw anything like it. Held the dice a good forty, forty five minutes."

"That was the unluckiest night of your life?"

"Yeah, because I made it that way, see? I was lucky but I didn't feel lucky. So I didn't put enough chips out there. Other guys at the table, they ironed the house flat. But all I took away was nine fifty. And I'll never have a roll like that again. Never."

"You got to be able to look at the odds," Tangeli said, "and then when you go for it, whatever happens, what the hell, it was a good bet."

"I know," Lasky said.

Tangeli's voice grew huskier, more thoughtful, giving his side-of-the-mouth delivery a poignant streetwise resonance. "I killed the gook who crippled me," he said. "Less . . . It was less than a second later. And it's helped. You know? Revenge is vastly underrated."

The soprano approached them with her donation can. "Thanks guys. Sorry we had to start over on that note."

They both dropped in bills. "That's okay, kid," Lasky said. "I've started over on lots of notes."

"Try us again next week—Mozart and Verdi," she said, moving on.

"Course you got certain people always gonna figure I shoulda been happy with that nine fifty," Tangeli said. "And maybe they're right. Maybe you ought to be satisfied scraping around on the bottom of things. But me, I look at the guys on top, and I figure they're not any smarter than me."

"Yeah, but they're lucky," Lasky said.

"You're right about that, kid. Being lucky. That's what it's all about. It's more important than money, talent, brains, . . . Luck is everything."

"Lucky thing for you," Lasky said.

Tangeli smiled.

"Forty thousand's a lot more than nine fifty, Bobby," Lasky said. He bought two more beers from the vendor.

"You know, kid," Tangeli said, "you're gonna end up dead whether you keep the money or not. Eventually I mean, right? But eventually might not get here for forty years. You were dealt a good hand. So play your cards. But whatever you do, don't run."

"Okay." Lasky agreed. One backward step and they'd be all over him like red-eyed dogs.

Lasky wished he'd known someone like Tangeli before he talked his way onto Wall Street and then kicked all those holes in his resume. The skills he'd learned to survive as a kid turned out to be hindrances later on, enabling him to penetrate bourgeoisie life but not succeed within it.

"But I have to ask myself," Lasky said. "What would I do with all that cash, anyway?"

"I don't know, kid. Tell you the truth, I don't know myself. Use your imagination, I guess. But what I'm trying to tell you . . .forty large, it'll keep you in action, sure, if action's all you want. But playing just to play, that's for suckers. What it's all about is winning. Winning's the best. Try it. If you don't like it, you can always go back to losing."

Lasky watched a point somewhere above Tangeli's head, not daring to meet his eyes, and for the first time he understood just how desperately he wanted his approval. He tried to empty his voice of feeling. "You figure I'm a loser," he said.

Replied Tangeli, "Loser's not what I meant. Dumb's what I meant." They both laughed, making it all right again. "What'd Dylan call it? Gargling in the rat-race choir. Well, you could a done that. You could a done that easy. You just didn't play their game, that's all. Besides, women love fuckups. Hey, you're an ass kicker, good buddy. You don't have to let the wiseguys run over you. You went to Harvard, remember?"

"Not that it matters now, but I went to Boston University.

I took summer courses at Harvard. Beavis and Butthead could take summer courses at Harvard."

In his last job as an ass kicker, he worked in a nondescript corner of an inconsequential government office with tired yellow walls and little gray metal desks. It all had the stench of a forgotten vessel stuck on the bottom of nowhere. Tangeli was right. Failure, particularly stupendous, glaring failure, was vastly more romantic than mediocrity. Perhaps that's why going from table to table felt better than going from job to job.

# CHAPTER EIGHT

# Pretty Woman in the Morning

Grinder, peering over the rim of his coffee cup past the Dentist, noticed Stalisi was even more ragged this morning. Two nights in a row with the Dentist and his bird-shit pals in their birdshit cop bars could take it out of anybody. Everybody buying rounds for the genuine Chicago wiseguy.

Grinder hated cop bars, never had much use for other cops. Police departments basically attracted civil-service mentalities. His fellow cops were almost without exception boring flunkies who started tallying their pension points at age twenty-two. The rest were dangerous loonies like Joe.

"I don't understand why this Lasky merits so much tip-toeing around," Stalisi said. The three of them sat at a well-appointed table on the mezzanine overlooking the gaming area of the Shangri-la. The tables below were only lightly sprinkled with customers who played in the drowsy, quiet manner of morning gamblers.

"It's the smart thing to do," Grinder explained once more. "Lasky's got friends. If they say they'll put the money in circulation, believe it. Meanwhile, the pressure's on him."

"You want them to get away with it?" Stalisi said evenly.

There it was, starting again. You couldn't make peace with this guy. "Get away with what?" Grinder said. "The money's not going anywhere."

"For Christ's sake, they're laughing at you. They're laughing at me."

Grinder stubbed out a butt he'd forgot he even lit. "Mr. Stalisi," he said, "time's on our side, believe me. He's the one with the worries."

"Bullshit. *We* got worries, he's got the sandwich."

"No, I don't think so. He just knows something about it, probably where it's at. But he's not spending it, and he's not enjoying life these days. He's in a corner. We just need a little time to make him realize it. But you want to get rid of him? Be my guest. I'm easy. Just don't tell me about it. And be sure you get the three million first."

"This Lasky, he's half-Jew, right?" Stalisi said.

"What I understand. But you go in Saturday, I don't think you'd find him in a synagogue."

"How well does Bitsy know him?" Stalisi said.

"Bitsy? He circumcised him, that's how far back they go."

"You kidding me?"

"Yes, I'm kidding you," Grinder said. "I don't think they ever spoke to each other in their lives. But if you think Bitsy's double-crossing anybody . . ."

"Nah, I didn't say that," Stalisi said. "Just trying to size things up, that's all. We don't want to be surprised."

"Course not."

"But from what I hear, it's this Tangeli who's helping him out. He'd be the one who Lasky must a told where the cash is. 'Cause he had to tell somebody."

"Right," Grinder agreed.

"Otherwise," Stalisi said, "he couldn't be threatening what'll happen to the money if we fuck with him. He might not even know where the money is anymore. It might be this Tangeli who knows."

"That's true," Grinder said. Could it be that this prick was fishing information out of the Dentist? It didn't seem possible. Maybe the Dentist sucked up to the guineas, but he'd always understood what it meant to be partners. Grinder looked over at the Dentist, but except for anger, Joe never revealed much in his face. If he were a little smarter, he could be a poker ace.

"So what about this Tangeli?" Stalisi said. "He buddied up with somebody? With Bitsy maybe?"

"Stop asking me about Bitsy, okay?" Grinder said. "You want to know, he'll be here soon enough. Ask him."

"Fine," Stalisi said.

A security guard approached, bringing over the Lasky broad and her boy gofer. "Glad you could make it," Grinder said.

She answered all sweet and business at the same time. Grinder loved pretty women in the morning. Less than an hour ago, she'd been putting on her undies, studying herself in the mirror. What a slim, tidy thing she was. The smart ones were always hotter. Grinder introduced Joe and Stalisi. He said Stalisi represented the insurance company.

❀

Leno joked about Al Gore. *The Tonight Show* audience howled. Bitsy smiled. An early riser, he always taped the show and watched the next morning. Just then a security guard approached him in the eye-in-the-sky room. "Mr. Rossman—"

Bitsy held up his hand for quiet. He saw something he didn't like on one of the surveillance monitors. Killing the sound on Leno, he called for Nestor, who bounced over like a soufflé, his shirt halfway out of his pants and his gut spilling over.

"Watch this guy on first base," Bitsy said. "Screen Number Two."

Nestor studied Number Two. A top view of a table with two players. The guy at first base wore an Australian bush hat. Next to him was the sourpuss embezzler who hung around Bob Tangeli's place. Counting down the shoe again.

"Zoom in on the Aussie," Bitsy said. "Now the dealer. . . .Okay, back to the long shot. . . .Well?"

After maybe two whole minutes, Nestor answered. "I didn't see anything there, Mr. Rossman. The guy's playing greens, but his plays are . . .He looks kosher to me. Now the guy next to him, he—" He zoomed in on the professor.

"Forget the guy next to him," Bitsy said.

"But—"

"I said forget him. Sure, he counts, but he plays nickels. We couldn't buy a shill with what that schlemiel takes away. He's a bargain."

"You're the boss," Nestor said, switching back to the customer in the bush hat. "What's going on? This guy maybe playing with the house?"

"Nah, dealer's clean," Bitsy said. "But Mr. Aussie, he's . . ." He watched carefully, turning his head at an angle. "Maybe got a computer. Quarter says he's a wrong customer."

"I'll just go a nickel. That he's not wired," Nestor said.

Bitsy smiled. "You got a bet. We don't need any more. Move in." He turned to the guard. "Okay, what?"

"Grinder says they're waiting for you on the mezzanine, Mr. Rossman."

Grinder and Joe the Dentist rose to greet Bitsy. Joe even gave the old guy a hint of a smile. Bitsy held out his hand, smiling with sturdy old yellow teeth. "Laura Lasky, right?" he said, shaking her hand.

Grinder watched Laura and her gofer appraise the tall, skeletal Bitsy. Skin splotched with acne scars, age spots, some freckles from his youth. But he still moved like the young man he was when he pitched two years in the minors, seven weeks with Cincinnati before they sent him down for the shoulder.

Laura introduced the Fetherling kid, who offered his hand and tried to pull one of those finger-squeeze acts on Bitsy. The old man brought up his big left hand and dug a thumb deep into a pressure point on the kid's wrist. The kid let go like his hand was on fire. A good man to watch, Bitsy.

The waiter immediately brought over an orange juice served in a glass of thick crystal and a steaming coffee. "We have whitefish today, Mr. Rossman. Very fresh," the waiter said.

"Just bring us a selection" Bitsy said. "You know how to do it."

As the waiter nodded and left for the kitchen, Grinder

spotted a drama playing itself out in the gaming area below them. One by one, everyone else did, too. Four security guards approached a dude with a ponytail under his Australian bush hat. They spoke with him briefly. Then he rose, placed his chips in his pockets, and escorted by the guards, calmly made his way toward the office at the far end of the room.

Everything looked civilized until suddenly the Aussie made a break, running over a cocktail waitress like a fullback through cellophane. A pit boss tried to corner him as the four security guards gave chase. Without hesitating, the man leaped onto a craps table and ran down its length, stunning three players and the dice crew. He jumped down to a slot-machine aisle, knocking aside players and their cups of coins.

Bitsy asked the broad, "You had a comfortable night?" He liked this.

"Very comfortable," she said. "What did that man do?"

"He cheated," Bitsy said. "Anyway, let's get down to business. It's like Grinder told you. An armored car carrying a delivery from this casino was hijacked. And the detectives here suspect your ex-husband may be an accomplice."

"After the fact," Grinder said.

"Right, after the fact," Bitsy said. "Now . . ."

"Excuse me," she interrupted. "But I find that very interesting. That you'd call me. Whose idea was it to call Wisconsin?"

"You forget?" Grinder said. "Bitsy didn't call you. I did."

"Excuse me. You're right of course. But—"

"It was my idea," Grinder said.

"But why? Why did you think to call me?"

"When I need to find a guy, or maybe just convince him,

I look for his old cellmates. It's a percentage play. Always worth a try."

"Cellmate?" she laughed.

"Sure, cellmates, ex-wives . . .whatever."

She looked at Grinder with new appreciation. Grinder could get used to her fast.

"And we appreciate your dropping everything to help out," Bitsy said. "It's the right thing to do. Because this Lasky, he's not cooperating." The old man paused. "And that could be very bad for him. As for us, we just want our cargo back. If you could help us, it would be very good for your husband, in the long and the short run."

"Ex-husband," the broad corrected him.

Grinder spotted a fifth security guard at the end of the aisle, ready to grab the man in the Aussie hat. The fugitive smashed into him, arms flailing. As they grappled on the floor, two of the pursuing guards reached them. One thunked their prey low on the legs with his baton. The other Maced him in the face. He flopped around now like a fish in the dirt. These casino guards were well-trained, not your typical rent-a-cops. Man for man, they were probably better than the uniforms Grinder had to work with.

They yanked at the man's clothes, revealing a set of wires taped to his chest. Grinder knew they would lead down to his shoes, where he worked the controls with his toes. The cops dragged him, unresisting now, back toward the office.

"They tell me you got some kind of organization you're putting together," Bitsy said. "Tell me about it."

The Aussie down below, reaching the office door, elbowed one guard in the face and tripped down the other, exploding in renewed fury as he resumed his dash toward the revolving doors.

"Guy's got a set a balls, doesn't he?" Grinder said.

Still another cop, arms in a wrestling stance, stepped out to confront the player. The man sailed into him, downing him with a quick, beautifully executed head butt. He resumed running. Just a few yards from the revolving door, a middle-aged oriental dealer stuck out her little foot.

Contact. The guy flew for awhile, his feet in motion like a cartoon character running off a cliff. When he came down, his head struck hard against the foundation of the blackjack table. The guards were on him in a second. One of them smacked him in the head with a baton once, twice, three times. Another cuffed him, and they dragged him, semiconscious, toward the office again.

"At what point do they read him his rights?" the Lasky woman said.

"After we bury him," Bitsy said.

"That device he had in his shoe," Grinder explained, "it's a felony to use one of those in a casino."

"But it doesn't actually change the cards, does it?" she said. "As I understand it, it just helps him play better."

"Like I said, he's a thief," Bitsy explained. "We didn't twist his arm to come in here with that thing. You shouldn't worry about him. How come you people are always so worried about what happens to criminals?"

"You people?" she said.

"Yeah, you people," Bitsy said.

"I wouldn't be so quick to categorize others," she said in a civil tone.

"Listen," Bitsy said, "all these animals out on the streets? If they're crazy, they're crazy like a fox. 'Cause they don't try any of their crap in here. Sure, we get counters, con artists like this guy, crossroaders, we call them. But nobody hurts our customers."

"They had this case over in California—" Stalisi said.

"Mr. Stalisi is an attorney," Bitsy said. "Excuse me, Lou."

"Sure," Stalisi said. "I just wanted to say that Mr. . . . Bitsy's got a point."

"If the Founding Fathers faced the kind of shit we do every day," Bitsy said, "believe me, they'd know what to do."

"This case in California," Stalisi said, "the defendant cut somebody's head off. I mean he whacked it off. ACLU said nobody proved his intent was to murder. So they rescinded the sentence. He almost walked altogether. Can you believe that?"

Whenever Grinder heard wiseguys making a stand for law and order, which was not unusual, he felt perhaps he was living in a looney bin.

"Maybe they figured it was a shaving accident," Joe said.

"Exactly," Bitsy said. "Meanwhile, you got these Republican sonsofabitches in their country clubs, what a they do about all this shit? Nothing. They talk a lot of shit, but it's just talk. 'Cause if you lock everybody up who needs locking up, you put all the crazies in mental institutions, it takes a lot of taxes, and that's against their religion, right? So basically, we're on our own. It's not the cops' fault. Good cops, hard-working cops like Grinder and Joe, they do what they can. But they get no support and they've got to watch every step. So in here, we got basically one rule. Don't fuck with us. If you'll excuse the expression."

The broad did not look shocked.

"This is something everybody can understand," Bitsy said. "Our customers, they tell us all the time how safe they feel in here. We got little old ladies walking around with fists full a black chips. Nobody touches them. Believe me."

"Tell that to the man your guards just dragged away," she replied.

Bitsy just smiled. He liked smart broads, too, even when they were bitches. The waiter, assisted by a second server, brought over two carts of scrambled eggs, toast, fresh rolls, smoked fish, bacon, fresh fruit, and raw vegetables. They put together a modest plate for Bitsy, then filled requests for each of those at the table. Grinder knew he was going to eat too much. The Dentist ate nothing at all. Acting like some kind of Apache. Always putting on a show.

A technician from upstairs came over. Smiling, he handed Bitsy a five-spot, whispered something inaudible in his ear, then left.

Bitsy asked Laura again about her phony political organization.

"Solutions America," the Fetherling guy jumped in. "It's predicated on implementing whatever is needed, without regard to liberal or conservative concepts. We've had a tremendous response so far. People want answers, not rhetoric. They're not afraid to step on toes, and so we operate just like they do. Without concern for special interest groups. Basically, Solutions America is the reason we're here. This is part of a Western swing, to get the word out."

Lasky's ex-wife hadn't mentioned any plans to come out here when Grinder called her. In fact, she even mentioned she'd have to make arrangements. But he let it go. Let the kid make his lying little noises.

Said the Lasky broad, "What we're trying to do is take those concepts we've used in Madison that we know work—concepts on housing, jobs, health in the workplace—see if we can share them with other communities."

"Whenever applicable," Fetherling said.

"Sounds beautiful," Bitsy said. "Only I don't have much use for politics. Personally speaking."

"Who does?" she said. "But no matter how you define it,

politics isn't the enemy. It's just an expression of how civilization is organized. I'm sure you have politics right here in this casino. You just call it something else, that's all. But you know, I believe you have some very interesting ideas, Mr. Rossman. We could use your help—to keep us honest."

"You're a lovely, very intelligent young woman," Bitsy said. "I like talking to you. But you see, whatever success we have, it's got nothing to do with government. The only thing good about the government is when it leaves us alone."

Bitsy leaned closer to her. "Let me tell you a secret. They say I was one a the biggest bookmakers in Cleveland? Well it's bullshit. Listen, I ran a small operation. Cops used to say I sold appliances as a front. Hell, that was no front. That was 'cause I had to make a living. 'Cause I didn't have the connections. Now—" he gestured with one hand as though showing off a splendid sculpture, his beloved casino "—I don't need connections anymore. 'Cause I built this, understand? And government had nothing to do with it. Connections neither."

"You're being humble," Laura said. "From what I hear, you're connected to some very powerful people indeed."

Bitsy laughed. "Look, why don't we stop bullshitting each other?" he said.

"Fine," she said, turning to Stalisi. "You didn't mention the name of your firm."

Stalisi beamed with pride. Guys who were mobbed up figured it made them a hit with the babes.

"Look, I was kind of kidding you," Bitsy said. "About politics, I mean. Fact is, I hear you're doing excellent work. We'd be very appreciative if you can help us with our problem. And there would be a finder's fee, of course."

"From our firm," Stalisi said.

"I'm sure Grinder mentioned it to you," Bitsy said.

The Fetherling guy and Laura each searched the other's face for signals. Then Laura turned away fast, aware of being watched, caught in an old poker trick. Now Grinder was absolutely certain Fetherling was poking her. What a waste of talent.

"That's what I wanted to talk to you about," she told Bitsy. "The finder's fee. But I'm not sure this is the time or place."

Bitsy ignored this. "From what I hear of your ex-husband," he said, "if he's in on this, there's no telling what he might do next. Which could force us to act. And we don't want that. He's an attorney. He has a lot to lose. Try to make him understand. All we're looking for is to get our cargo back. You find out something, drop a dime. We'll make you glad."

"How glad is that?" Laura said.

"Forty thousand," Bitsy said.

She opened her mouth to protest.

Bitsy said, "It's our money, sweetheart. We won it fair and square."

# CHAPTER NINE

# Dentist Pliers

When Lasky gave him the address of the housing project, the cab driver suddenly decided he was out of service. Finally he agreed to make the trip for an extra ten-spot, but he was still surly about it. In this town, sometimes even bribes wouldn't buy courtesy. The driver peeled away while Lasky was still closing the door. Not auspicious.

He was sorry he'd wasted time picking up the Chinese food. Already an eerie darkness was settling over the place, even as heat blistered the surrounding concrete and asphalt like a hair dryer from hell.

Lasky walked through a pitted parking lot littered with broken glass and junk cars with makeshift security chains attached to their hoods. Kids were everywhere, making lots of noise. Wild kids.

The eight building exteriors were festooned with washing, giving them the appearance of rag monsters. As he drew closer to an entrance, a thousand radios and stereos blared more intense. Like a prison tier, Lasky realized.

When government built the project, high-rise housing for the poor had been a failed, sunken strategy for more than thirty years. Its only real supporters were the layers of hacks and fixers who made a killing off the land deal and construction kickbacks. Vegas was like that. From its very beginning, the city thrived on dead concepts.

Lasky had some directions, but they were useless. The buildings all looked alike, and there were no addresses anywhere. He headed for a group of young men playing half-court basketball in the near-darkness. They grunted and sweated as though their lives rode on the outcome. A little girl wandered onto the court, and somebody ran her over. The game went on as an older girl dashed out and pulled her away, crying.

Lasky halted at the doorway. It looked more like an underground parking entrance than the door to a high-rise. Around the frame, graffiti was scrawled on top of graffiti, years and years of it, all in the angular, neurotic characters that the scrawlers never seemed to vary over time.

Three teenagers sat on a bike rack that held no bikes. Lasky asked them for directions.

"Whutchoo doing here, man?" one of them said. "You a cop?"

"Ain't no cops walking around here alone," a second kid said. "Hey, you looking for them TV guys? They left already."

"I'm handing out money, is what I'm doing," Lasky said. He offered two bucks for an escort to the right apartment. The kids bargained awhile, and they settled on two now, two later. Had he offered them ten they'd demand twenty.

"You at the wrong entrance, man," the second kid finally told Lasky. He was short and stocky with an expansive face. He blinked too much, probably from nerves. It made him appear thoughtful. He led Lasky away. After awhile, he said, "I'll show you, but I ain't going up."

"That's not the deal," Lasky said.

The kid stopped, then Lasky. "That ain't my building," the kid said. "You're the dude wants inside."

"I'm not asking you to live there," Lasky said. "I'm paying you to show me the right apartment."

"I'm the wrong set, man."

"There's only one set here," Lasky said. "Everybody knows that."

"Everybody knows that," the kid said in derision. "Look man, there's sets, and there's sets. And there's sets inside the sets. I ain't got time to lay it all out. What if I was a white boy wearin' a hundred-dollar shirt? Would you be tryin' to send me in there for a lousy four bucks? It's dangerous, man."

Lasky surrendered. "Just give me good directions after you show me the entrance, okay?"

They recommenced walking. "Bet you're going to see those lame-ass whiteys live up here," the kid said.

"Tell you the truth, kid, I don't know what color they are. I never met them."

"Hey, I ain't your kid. You know you look like one a them bounty hunters, maybe. You should be giving me a split."

"What's your name?"

"Don't get queer on me, dude."

"I ain't your dude," Lasky said. "You know, you shouldn't be such a hardass to someone who's paying you for a favor."

They argued, not seriously, over who was doing whom a favor. Finally the kid stopped in front of a building on the perimeter and gave Lasky detailed instructions. "Remember man," he said, "stay outa that elevator."

As Lasky climbed the dark, concrete stairs inside, TVs and other amplified sounds intensified and receded along the way. At the third-floor landing, he passed a bag lady of indeterminate age who paid him no notice as she scrubbed clothes in an old tub. Her eyes were big, brown, and intelligent.

On the next floor, he turned down a long passageway. The light splashed more vague and infrequent along the gritty cinder-block walls of the littered hallway. TV noises gave way to obtuse sounds and echoes, like a lonely subway station at night. Advancing cautiously, he heard people conversing up ahead—telltale voices of delight and dejection. He came upon a hallway crap game.

Seven shadows froze, watching the white man who didn't belong. Cop? Rip-off artist? Social worker? Finally satisfied there was no threat, the players forgot about him.

Rounding a corner, Lasky heard the kind of snarl that emanates from an animal that intends to kill you. He froze. He saw it now, a pit bull tearing, straining at a chain, jumping into the air and coming down choked, angrier. The dog patrolled an area outside a metal door.

Beyond was almost total darkness. He moved cautiously along the wall, feeling it with his fingertips as he left the terrible sound of the dog behind him. After another twenty yards, he bumped into something live and jumped backward. Someone switched on an overhead light.

At least two people were sitting along the wall. Two others stood over a man in a dark face who leered at Lasky, toothless, as he crouched on his haunches, shooting dope into a vein in his leg. Lasky became aware of a sewer odor.

"Back off," a voice said.

"It's him," said another.

Lasky moved around the junkies.

"Hold it, man," a drowsy voice said. "You got a toll to pay. This our house, un'erstand? Can't go walkin' through a man's house."

The light went out again, and a form burst forward, lunging at Lasky with something in its hand. He skipped away, catching the blow on his shoulder. The Chinese food hit the floor.

Lasky kicked at the man with the needle. His shoe sank into scrawny flesh, and he felt better. A fight was always less terrifying than the anticipation of a fight. He pulled his pistol and clutched a clump of hair with his other hand, jamming the pistol against the face.

Somebody blindsided him. A pair of hands caught the little finger of his gun hand and bent it back. The pistol clattered to the floor. Lasky punched wildly at whomever was bending his finger. He tore his hand free, but then something heavy thudded along the side of his neck. He felt himself fading into The Room, a dark place Muhammed Ali once described, where bats blew saxophones in your ear while you slid into their looney, slow-motion cadence.

But Lasky's senses screamed back, throbbing with the power of his fear. He stepped to the side and hooked a couple hard lefts into his attacker's liver. He missed him with a knee and lost his balance but managed to stay on his feet. Now he could make out the face of the one who'd tackled him. He was a white man, with long hair tied in a bun, giving him the appearance of a plain, middle-aged woman.

Enraged, the man rushed in like a skinny offensive guard. He held something in his hand now. Lasky intercepted it with both hands and felt something slice his palm like a loaf of pastrami. He hissed a yell through his teeth while another junky, maybe the toothless one, grabbed him from behind. Lasky twisted the skinny one's razor hand as someone pummeled him with weak punches. One of his opponents smelled like bad potatoes.

Lasky threw elbows into the gut behind him, then leaped onto the one with the razor, shooting a forearm into his throat, feeling it slide under the chin. The man sank to his knees, emitting a terrible rattle. Lasky had the razor now. Gorged on pain and fear, he whirled and sliced the other man across the face with his left hand. There was no shriek of pain. He acted like his face was just a rubber mask.

Lasky's foot touched his pistol. He picked it up and fired into the air. In this corridor, it sounded like a howitzer. As he swung around, he saw his attackers running into the darkness.

Lasky searched for the Chinese food. One of the bags' contents were scattered. He couldn't find the hot and sour soup. "Shit," he said.

He knew he must be thinking in a fog, searching for take-out cartons while his right hand was sticky with blood. He found a new crease in the palm of his right hand. He tried to tear a bandage from the bottom of his shirt, but both hands were weak and shaking. Finally he realized he should put down the two bags of food first.

"You do fair against stumblebums, mouse," a voice called out.

Lasky ducked into a crouch. "Nice to hear from you, Joe," he replied into the darkness.

"You trembling, mouse? Sounds like you're trembling."

"Fuck you." All he could think of for now. He couldn't

see where Joe the Dentist was, but he was close. "Those friends of yours?" Lasky said. "Or relatives, maybe."

"I mighta given them a couple bucks so they wouldn't hurt me," the Dentist's voice said. He laughed a phony, hard laugh. "Why? You think you're the only nickel-and-dimer on the take? You know, when I was a kid, there was this nigger, I liked him about the way I like you, he got in a lucky punch one time, knocked out one a my teeth. What I did, I hunted him down, pulled his teeth out with a pliers. Should a heard the screams. He was one unhappy nigger. You never should a stuck a gun in my face, know what I'm saying? Hey, what's the matter, sheenie? Ain't got no snappy comebacks?"

Lasky tightened his grip on the pistol. "Awfully sweet of you to share your childhood memories, Joe. You lurking out there for any particular reason?"

"Damn! You mean the Number Six bus doesn't go through here?"

Lasky didn't like the fact that the Dentist wouldn't show himself. He heard someone slide the action on a gun, probably a semiautomatic pistol.

"What was that?" the Dentist said happily.

Lasky figured the Dentist for a bluff, but still he hugged the wall like Garfield stuck to a car window. He wasn't sure, but he thought he saw somebody, maybe a couple people, crouched behind a discarded mattress not far away. He took off fast.

"See you soon, mouse," the Dentist called after him. About thirty yards down the passageway, Lasky stopped and poked under his makeshift bandage. It didn't look good. He debated making a tourniquet then decided against it. Better to bleed some then to contract blood poisoning. Meanwhile, his shaking subsided. But the bent finger on his sliced hand was swelling up fast.

He started back down the passageway. Around a corner, he saw the door he wanted and pounded on it. He heard steps. After a while, a voice behind the door asked him to identify himself. He did.

"How's it look out there?" the voice said.

"Like a week in the country," Lasky said. "You going to open up or what?"

There were sounds of locks and chains being unfastened, a crossbar removed. The door opened. There stood a thin, world-weary white man with awful posture who appeared to be in his fifties. His hair was a gray Brillo pad worn long to camouflage a hairline that receded to the back of his head like a wiry horseshoe.

"Doctor Livingston, I presume?" Lasky said.

The man ignored this, which put Lasky in his place. "Just wanted to make sure no one else was out there," he explained. Lasky entered and was struck by the smell of a cat box that hadn't been changed since the Colts played in Baltimore. The man rebolted the door quickly. Lasky followed him into a dark, cluttered apartment. No introductions. "What took you?" the weary man said.

"Picked up some Chinese," Lasky said to this man he'd never seen, handing him the bags. The man shouted back over his shoulder, "Leslie!"

"Did you know your place was being watched?" Lasky said.

"I said to come earlier, when the other entrance is open." The weary man yelled again, impatient, "Leslie!"

A kid about sixteen or seventeen ambled over grudgingly from another room somewhere. "Yeah," he said. The kid echoed precisely the weary voice and manner of his father. Same wire hair, only brown and full. Both of them gave the impression they were hanging from subway straps beneath Brooklyn, on their way someplace they didn't particularly want to go.

"Here, take this," the father said, handing over the bags of Chinese food.

The kid protested. Big imposition. Some kids were like that. The father led Lasky down a narrow hallway into a cramped, bohemian sort of sitting room where the cat box smell grew stronger and where eight skinny people sat around, most of them smoking. Four of them were on the floor crowded around a board game of Trivial Pursuit. Some of them smiled at Lasky. No introductions here either. At least the cigarette smoke camouflaged some of the cat-box smell.

The walls were covered with old photographs, Vietnam-era posters, and shelves of dusty, dusty books. The obligatory stereo played one of those preening modern classical compositions full of string instruments that sounded like they were all having a nervous breakdown.

When Lasky was a small boy traveling through Italy with his family, they had stayed awhile in a beat-up railroad hotel outside Venice. One warm night, Lasky dropped a toy car behind an old easy chair in the lobby. When he dropped down and slid his hand behind the chair to retrieve it, he touched forty years of dust and cobwebs, and his hand shrank back on its own, as though it had encountered the bony hand of death. This apartment reminded Lasky of that hotel.

The sorrowful-looking, prematurely cynical son followed after them, still acting like holding the brown bags of Chinese food was a uniquely hideous torture. The father grabbed the bags, then swept some junk off an end table onto the floor. Setting the bags down, he started removing cardboard cartons of food.

A player threw the dice. "Four, History." He moved his token.

"Good to see you, Terry," one of the skinny people said, approaching. It was Bags.

"Didn't recognize you," Lasky said, genuinely pleased to see him. "Anything to drink around here?"

The father found a bottle of Scotch and handed it to Lasky, who took a swig and passed it to Bags.

"Hey, what happened to your hand?" Bags said.

"Neighbors," Lasky told him.

"Jesus, let's take a look at that," Bags said.

"Let me," said the weary father. Without ceremony, he stuck his cigarette between his lips, grabbed Lasky's hand, and began unwrapping the bloody cloth around it. "Leslie," he said, "the kit." Exposed to the air, the wound hurt even worse. It itched, too.

The kid ambled back down the hall.

"Right away," the father said.

The kid ambled, same speed, into a doorway somewhere.

"Name Abraham Lincoln's wife," one of the Trivial Pursuit players said.

Lasky got a quick look at his sliced hand before the weary father put pressure on the wound with the blood-soaked rag. Lasky took another swig of whiskey.

"This'll be okay," said the father. "Just keep pressure on it. But it'll have to be stitched up."

"Are you a doctor?" Lasky said.

"Generically speaking," the man answered. "I'm a doctor of philosophy."

"Tendons and everything all there?" Lasky said.

The man nodded half-heartedly, still studying the wound. He touched the bent finger, and Lasky winced. He watched the ash on the end of the man's cigarette, expecting it to fall into his wound any second.

A calico cat with one eye and a gray alley critter showed up. The calico, fascinated by the blood, rubbed its back along Lasky's arm. He shoved it away with the whiskey bottle.

"I know it, I know it," the Trivial Pursuit player said.

His partner thought aloud. "Lincoln's wife, Lincoln's wife . . .I got it! Jane Wyman!"

"Leslie, hurry the hell up, will you?" the father yelled.

"Sure it's not too bad?" Lasky said.

No answer. Not encouraging.

Finally the kid shuffled in with a metal suitcase, the kind used by professional photographers and cocaine smugglers. The father jerked it away and opened it to reveal a nicely stocked first-aid kit. He lined up contents next to the Chinese food cartons. "Did you see who was watching my place?" he said.

"Junkies," Lasky said.

"I thought we had a truce," the man said. "They don't bother us, and we don't call the cops. Maybe these're different ones. They still out there?"

"Hard to say," Lasky said. "They were probably looking for me."

"Why's that?" the weary man said. Getting no answer, he told Lasky, "You know, you look kind of like an undercover cop. That's not good."

"You mean I look like a cop who's trying not to look like a cop," Lasky said.

"You might say so," the weary man said. "I probably have some explaining to do to some of the neighbors."

"Look, they attacked me, get it? I didn't attack them. What's to explain?"

"That's the way things work around here sometimes," the weary man said. "Did you hurt anyone?"

"I hope so," Lasky replied.

The man shook his head. "This might hurt a bit," he said. He poured astringent on the wound. The pain traveled straight to a point behind Lasky's eyeballs. He let out an involuntary scream just as Laura entered from the hallway. She wore shorts and a white cotton blouse, buttoned low, no bra. Miles of leg. Cheerful and just a little sweaty.

"Could that be . . ." She sniffed the air " . . . Chinese food!"

She swooped up an egg roll, then threw herself at Lasky, hugging him around the neck, chewing.

"Kung pao shrimp," she said between bites. "You don't forget a thing, do you?" she mouthed in his ear. Suddenly startled, she let go of him. "You're bleeding. What happened?"

"Seems this is a bad neighborhood," Lasky said. "Got any of that egg roll?" She dug one out for him. Always efficient. "Go ahead, Doc," Lasky said. "This is a generic doc," he told Laura, then offered her a slug of whiskey. She found a glass, and he poured her a stiff shot.

"I think the finger's broken, too," the weary man said.

"You're not sure?" Lasky asked him.

"Can't be sure without an X-ray. It could be just a hyperextension. But we'll treat it like it's broken. Which it probably is. You'll have to get that wound sewed up though."

"Want a shot of this?" Lasky said to him.

He shook his head no. Lasky took another belt. "Not much left anyway."

Working quickly, the man stuck a splint on the finger and then bandaged over everything with gauze. The hand still hurt like deep hell, but Lasky felt calmer now.

"They can take care of this in an emergency room. Meanwhile, don't get it wet," the weary man said. "And get a tetanus shot." He gave two aspirins to Lasky, who thanked him. The man shrugged and killed the whiskey.

"C'mon," Laura beckoned Lasky.

# CHAPTER TEN

# Love So Sweet

Carrying what was left of the Chinese food, Laura led Lasky into a windowless room no bigger than a jail cell. Inside was a beat-up leather couch, a dust-caked hooked rug spread over a concrete floor, and an old wooden desk with a few books and papers scattered across its top. It all had a rarely used look. Fetherling appeared from somewhere and closed the door behind them, walling off the sound of the neurotic string instruments on the stereo.

The three of them devoured the food immediately. A solemn undertaking that proceeded without plates. They ate straight from the cartons like old friends. Lasky was proud of his beef in oyster sauce and Peking duck and fresh vegetables simmered in a mushroom sauce. Sure, Vegas was a vulgar town bereft of art, but it had terrific food.

"I thought maybe I could help you out of your predicament," Laura finally said, "and raise us some money in the bargain."

"Judging by your choice of hotels, I'd say you could use some," he said.

Fetherling smirked, triumphant. "You couldn't pay for the publicity we got staying here," he said. "You should have been here a few hours ago. We were up to our navels in TV cameras. You think they'd show up for a news conference at the Hilton?"

"It was good publicity for Ned, too," Laura said.

"Who's Ned?" Lasky asked her.

"Ned Warbell. This is his apartment," she said. Warbell, the man who dressed Lasky's wound, she explained, was a University of Nevada anthropologist doing a detailed study on the housing project and its residents.

"Think he'll find anything wrong?" Lasky said.

"Don't be so droll, sweetheart," Laura said. "If anyone's going to do anything substantive about the problems in places like these, the problems have to be documented first. Documented and brought to the public's attention. Then you go looking for help. You watch, he'll come up with some original findings. Maybe even some solutions. Ned has a good rapport down here."

"He worries about his rapport," Lasky said. "Says I screwed it up getting jumped in the corridor."

"Was it really just neighborhood people? Or did Bitsy Rossman get a little nasty?" Laura asked him.

"So you know about Bitsy," Lasky said.

"We get around some," Laura said. "He's got those two detectives in his hip pocket, and it's right out in the open. Some town you've got here."

"It's not just in Vegas," he said. "It's everywhere. Government's like this big restaurant, and maybe the working stiff pays the check but not the tip. Cops and politicians, they go elsewhere for that."

"And where would that be?" Laura said.

"Same places you go," Lasky said. "But in this town, it's to whoever owns the Strip. These new corporations wanted in, and they had the money, so they just built like crazy and elbowed the mob out of the way. Now Grinder, he's no different than the other cops. The difference is they answer to the new guys, and he and maybe a few others are still loyal to the old guys."

"But the old guys kill people," Laura said.

"Yeah, that's a problem," Lasky agreed.

"You sound almost like you admire them," Laura said.

"No," he said. "But at least they're more honest about their dishonesty."

"Do you think this Bitsy would really do something to you? Or is he a friend?"

"I don't even know him," Lasky said. He was getting angry with himself. Why was it so important to show up here when everything was hanging by a thread? Why did he care what Laura thought? "Look, I don't like being interrogated, okay? And don't roll your eyes to show your pal here you're dealing with some kind of lamentable asshole."

"You're right," she said. "It's obvious anyway" —getting a smile out of him. Laura showed her palms, an act of surrender. "I just asked if he's your friend, that's all."

"I don't have a lot of friends. Just like the old days, remember? When you wanted me to network."

It wasn't that Lasky actually disliked people. For the most part, he wished them well. But too many of them wanted to tell him more about themselves than he cared to hear. An attitude, he knew, that made him less than adored in some circles. Still, something made him want her to protest, to contradict him and say he was loved and admired by multitudes. She didn't.

She caught him staring at the familiar two-inch scar above her left ankle. It seemed to please her. She looked thoughtful now, like she was about to share a secret. "Why doesn't Bitsy just take the money away from you?" she said.

"What do you mean? Like torture me?" Lasky picked a book off the desk and absently leafed through it: *The Only Investment Guide You'll Ever Need*. This anthropologist must be a closet capitalist. Lasky skimmed some paragraphs on cyclical stocks. How to know when to take your profits. "Let me ask you something," he said. "Say you got your hands on some of that money. What difference would it make to you anyway?"

"I hear things," Laura said. "Madison's not far from Chicago, you know. I heard the kind of trouble you were in, and I knew how stubborn you can be. I didn't want them . . .I didn't want them to kill you, okay? I thought we might try to act as mediator. Maybe they'd be less likely to hurt you if we remind them I'm a superstar." Laura often laughed at her own notoriety. But Lasky knew that deep down she truly adored it.

"The sandwich you're after is the wrong side of legal," he said. "Even if you managed to get a piece, it would just blow up in your face."

"What sandwich?" she said.

"When the wiseguys skim some of the take from their casinos, before the IRS can count it, they'll call Chicago or New York or wherever it's going, and say, 'We've got a sandwich for you.' So that's what you're after. A sandwich. Along with my well-being, of course."

"You're still a cynical bastard," she said. She said it in a way that wasn't challenging. "Look, Terry, I want you to understand this isn't about me. It's about something much bigger. We're trying to accomplish something here."

"Unlike some people you could name," he said.

"Jesus, Terry, don't you care about anything anymore? Okay, so you hated your job. Couldn't you just look for a better one? There's lots to do out there. Did you look around here today? At the misery?" She raised her voice. "The children out there have no future, none of them—and they know it. Doesn't that bother you at all?"

"Since when were you interested in kids?" Lasky said.

"Don't start that," she said. Lasky watched her sharp, Scandinavian features dissolve from pretty into a hard, masculine visage, then back to pretty again. Her face did that sometimes.

It was awful to know there was someone like this, someone who knew you naked and mostly despised you. No wonder husbands and wives killed each other. He'd hated his job all right. But mostly because it forced him to come home to her each night as a loser. He'd been prosecuting interstate car thieves. Cretinous junkies, most of them, popping cars like so many capsules. They expected to do time once in a while, and they did. He was merely a minor functionary in a minor process, a notch or two below the insurance underwriters. Stuck on a pitiful team of sorry-ass lawyers who stank of failed longings like leftover cheese. They wore loser ties and loser haircuts, carried on loser conversations laced with third-rate witticisms. And he couldn't stand for Laura to see any of them.

"What you're saying, if I understand you right," he said, "is that if I let you con me out of some money, then I'll earn the right to feel warm and fuzzy."

Fetherling broke in again. "Even those of us trying to cut the ties between money and politics need money to get our message out. It's crazy, I know. But there it is. We have to scrounge."

"You mean like Lenin taking money from the Kaiser," Lasky said.

"Good analogy," said Fetherling. This guy was just too determined to be nice.

"Terry thinks he's superior to all this," Laura said, addressing Fetherling. "Our existential hero. Buried alive at a poker table."

Lasky stood up, ready to leave now. Fetherling stood up too, blinking and sweating in his casual jeans. He was beginning to look like a lost kid at a carnival. "Terry," he said, "I understand how you feel. But we've got all kinds of people working together on this. Look, I have to . . . I'm due somewhere else, okay? You two . . . Try to keep an open mind," he told Lasky, sticking out his hand for another one of those jerk handshakes, then muttering an excuse-me when Lasky wouldn't give him his bandaged hand. He cut out like he was late for his bar exam, shutting the door behind him.

Laura started packing up food cartons, placing them back in the bags like a good environmental soldier. Lasky could leave now. In fact, he never should have showed up. He sneaked another look at the white scar above her ankle.

"You always had a brutal side," she said after a while. "But you made love so sweetly, I could almost forget the other."

What the hell. He put his arms around her. They kissed. It was smooth and fun. New and full of memories.

"You're playing a lot of games here, Laurie. Too many games, too many schemes."

She removed her glasses then kissed him harder. Her

breath was husky from the Chinese food. It was hot in the windowless room.

"Just who is that errand boy of yours?" he asked her. They sat down on the leather couch. He started unbuttoning her blouse. It was difficult with his gimpy hand.

"Roy?" she said, kicking off her sandals. "You might call him chief of staff, only I'm stingy about giving out titles. And I'm not playing games. You can see that. I'm being open. Let me make a deal for you. Please."

"No way," he said.

"Bastard." Her blouse was off now. Red nipples taut, waistline still perfect. She unzipped his pants and kneeled before him. She freed his cock and began to stroke it, giving it all her attention. She'd always been a fast starter. He sank into the hot breath of her.

"You know," he finally blurted out, "I was kind of wondering what your chief of staff up there? Fetherling? What he preferred—you or the money . . . That was foolish, wasn't it?"

She stopped what she was doing and looked up at him coldly. She retrieved her blouse and began buttoning it furiously. "Get out," she said.

He didn't argue. But he had a bit of a struggle zipping up with a gimpy hand.

"Jesus, you're a bitter sonofabitch," she said.

"You know something?" he said. "Even when I know you're conning me, you make me feel guilty for not believing you. That's how good you are. But I guess you must know that. You know something else? You did, too." He rose and turned the doorknob. She looked at him quizzically. "You used to make love so sweet," he said.

Bags, peculiarly silent, drove him to a twenty-four-hour clinic, where a physician's assistant took an expensive X-ray and pronounced the finger sprained but unbroken. She sewed up the slice, gave him a shot, and sent him on his way.

Just before they reached Lasky's trailer, they passed a flabby woman of indeterminate age staring at a set of rusted railroad tracks, as though hoping to see a train bear down out of the darkness. When he was a boy, Lasky and his father used to get their hair cut in a sunny, crowded barbershop near the beach, where the tracks ran along the California coast. Everyone liked to stop what they were doing and look through the store window whenever a passenger train went by.

The barbers all smelled of cloves, and after Lasky's haircut, they would give him bubblegum. He would take it home to share with his sister. Maybe that night, if it were a Saturday, the family would go out for Thai food, and his sister would pick out her shrimps from the pad thai noodles and give them to Lasky. The restaurant kept a portrait of Thailand's royal couple on the wall. They looked open and generous and wore their ribbons and jewels with no hint of self-doubt. Nothing could touch them or their kingdom.

# Chapter Eleven

# Cable Cult

The Temple of Worth was a fat stucco oddity that hung low to the ground like an aspiring Pentagon. Acres of open space around the main building were surrounded by a paranoid, Alamo-like fence adorned with quack oriental spires. Maybe it was more like an idiot's Kremlin than a Pentagon, Lasky decided. A ranchero-style Kremlin.

Inside the main chapel, Pinky lectured to an audience of perhaps 150. He stood, both hands on the lectern, clutching a cigarette. On the stage behind him were arrangements of flowers and shelves of mostly whacky books he consulted from time to time during his preaching. Off to one side were a jumble of television cameras and a crew of three. Off to the other were five choir members in pink robes and a seven-piece country band. Lasky, making his way in toward the back of the hall, saw the drummer sneak a quick pull of booze from a small decanter behind the bass drum.

The audience was mostly made up of the kind of people who were ardently pursued by time-share sales reps. They were bookkeepers, waitresses, forklift operators, all of them looking for some place to turn. This was a special introductory lecture, and so only a few hard-core dressed-for-success Pinks were sprinkled among the new fish.

Lasky, who hoped he'd missed most of the lecture, came in as Pinky scolded the world for its lousy attitude toward opportunity, then recounted how he'd risen from a family of coal-country losers into "a world of success, a world of fame and financial independence," and how he lost it all, then rose from the ashes of devastation to success again. Divorce, bankruptcy, false charges, they're just obstacles. You climb them, go around, or through. "You get past, that's all."

"Look to the ancients. Abraham, Moses, Christ, Buddha. Heavy rollers, every one of them," Pinky said in the half-shout of his lectern voice. "They laid everything out there on the Pass Line and let 'er rip. By God, they didn't snivel around worrying about what they lost or what they should have won before. We know what that game is. It's a loser's game."

At that point Pinky spotted Lasky and winked. "And sure, the prophets, they knew about losers, 'cause they're something that's always been around. Suckers playing one long shot after another, or suckers who won't play at all. These people have always been around. They're nothing new. But the heavy hitters? No, they're never tempted by the comfort of loss . . .the ease of regret."

He paused here and slowly scanned the audience members. One by one, they lowered their gaze. They were his. His people. He probably even loved them. "Because nobody's got anything to regret," he said in a slower, softer cadence. "There's no time," he half-whispered. He shook his head and smiled. A pause for emphasis, then a return to full voice.

"The prophets, they always look forward, not back. And mind you, when giants walked the Earth, their world was just as modern to them as ours is to us. Don't you see? No one's ever really lived in ancient times. Ancient's what folks who come later call it. Everyone lives in modern times. King David, Buddha, Jesus, Mohammed, and now us. Think about it. In an Earth as young as ours, isn't it blasphemy to feel sorry for ourselves 'cause maybe we can't get our hands on a bunch a junk's gonna be outmoded next year anyway when Japan ships over a new pile? Am I right?"

Lasky wasn't sure what point Pinky was trying to make, but the words seemed to please the spectators, many of whom nodded in recognition of some basic truth, a kind of savage epiphany that brought them comfort.

Pinky turned and browsed through the volumes behind him as though he had no audience. Then he slowly returned to the lectern and placed his lips against the microphone to shout a name, "Saul of Tarsus!" He nodded knowingly, as though sharing a cheerful secret. "Saul of Tarsus—did he waste his time lamenting the passing of what had gone before?"

Heads shook no. Pinky smiled. "Heck no. And just look what he missed. Had he been born only forty years earlier—a millisecond of time in our vast universe—he could have known his Lord in the flesh. Not a vision, but flesh, the Lord in the flesh."

"Because he knew, yes, in his secret heart, he knew, the odds a meeting Jesus in the great over yonder? Well, it's just a proposition bet, ain't it? By God, what happened to Saul of Tarsus, the man who became the blessed Saint Paul, is he missed the jackpot by the width of one little chip. But did he give up? Did he fold his cards? Just lay down and die? Well? Whattaya think?"

Scattered shouts of "No!"

"Damn right, he didn't. He played the hand he was dealt, didn't he? And before long, he was just pulling in one pot after another until sweet Jesus, he raked one in the size of a damn Oldsmobile, if you'll excuse my expression."

Laughter, nodded heads.

"And meanwhile, here you sit, some of you, crying over your American Express Gold Card or Gucci or Pucci or whatever it is you tell yourself you just got to have. Brothers, sisters, the thing to do now, the thing for all of us to do, is to forget what's been lost. What you did wrong or what maybe didn't work out the way you'd liked. I'll bet . . .If any a you are like I was, I'll bet you could name every rotten choice you ever made, can't you? Every single mistake. Am I right or not?" he smiled.

Appreciative laughter from the audience.

"Course you can. We're great at punishing ourselves, aren't we? All of us running around with a catalog of nasty deeds and bad decisions to whip ourselves with. Well, I'm here to tell you, forget it! You hear me? Just throw all a that stuff out of your mind, once and for all. All those properties you should a bought and didn't, all those deals you should of avoided and didn't. Remember eight-hundred-dollar gold? Hell, I remember *buying* eight-hundred-gold." A round of new laughter.

"But I don't let it bother me, all those bad bets . . .And forget the people you disappointed. Especially forget that. Sounds cruel? Well think about this, then. Don't . . .disappoint . . .yourself."

"But let's get specific, okay? Here's what you do. Here's

what we do at the Temple of Worth. Like Saul of Tarsus, we just raise us a new bankroll. We begin to understand what it is that's really worth having in this cockeyed world, and then we get out there and help each other to get it. We get it together, that's what we do. We dedicate ourselves, and we help ourselves. We set ourselves free and allow ourselves—to . . ." He cupped a hand to his ear.

"Win!" shouted back the hard-core Pinks.

"Say what?" said Pinky, joyfully.

"Win!" said the audience, louder now, as neophytes joined in.

"Like you mean it, now," Pinky coached them.

"Win." Louder still.

"By God, I'm talking about it all!"

"Win!"

"Having it all!"

"Win!"

"Now I hear you—"

"Win!"

"By God, I do hear you!"

"Win!"

"You do mean it!"

Now Pinky and his audience built a faster cadence, shouting together: "Win! . . .Win! . . .Win! . . .Win! . . .Win! . . .Win! . . .Win! . . .Win! . . ."

Pinky raised both his arms and let the audience take it alone: "Win! . . .Win! . . .Win! . . .Win! . . .Win! . . .

He brought his arms down abruptly, the signal for the band, which broke into "Gather at the River." The enthralled audience ceased chanting. Its members laughed and cried in relief, looking about, sharing the wonder.

Pinky smiled a smile of conquest. "Bow your heads," he said, dropping his cigarette to the floor and stepping on it.

The band stopped playing, and the audience obeyed. Pinky signaled to Lasky, pointing toward a side door. Lasky crossed toward it as three ushers carrying collection trays lined up in the rear of the aisles. Behind each usher was a cute, stewardess-looking assistant wheeling along a cart carrying an assortment of instructional audiotapes, engraved cigarette lighters, and other inspirational items.

"Lord," Pinky began, "have mercy on these loving souls. Show them the way. Help me to show them the way. Remove the barriers to their dreams of plenty and heal their wounds. For they do grieve, Lord. Please comfort them in their pain and bring them—"

Lasky slipped into a large office and closed the door behind him. He'd had occasion to enter only a couple times before. The office had been decorated by a pro. Lots of polished wood in medium tones. The walls were covered with plaques and signed photographs, most of them of a happy-faced Pinky posing with various celebrities and moneyed potentates. There were shots from both his author days and his postliterary spiritual life.

A pouty, very pretty young woman in gray slacks and a checkered shirt shot pool alone in the corner. She paid no attention to Lasky as he mixed himself a drink at an executive bar.

Over on Pinky's desk, he spotted what appeared to be astrological charts with calculations penciled neatly all over them. A melancholy display of faith. As far as Lasky knew, Pinky never included astrology in his preaching. Perhaps he was philosophically opposed to revealing anything he actually believed himself. Lasky idly watched the young woman shoot pool for a minute or so, and then Pastor Pinky charged in like an Olympic walker.

"Good to see you, Terry. Chris take care a you, all right?"

Pinky seated himself on a silky leather loveseat, and Lasky sat down across from him in a matching easy chair. The young woman, smiling now, handed her boss a drink. "Bet you walked right past the donation box again," Pinky chuckled.

Lasky's attention now was on Chris, the pretty young woman. Suddenly he was unsure of Chris's gender. The face and form alternated. He could convince himself of one conclusion, then the other. Both were absolutely plausible. The earring, the clothes, the hair, the movement, the voice, the name were all alternating mysteries. Like the face of his ex-wife changing from breathtaking beauty to the hard visage of a Viking plunderer, then back.

Sometimes two contrasting sets of facts failed to cancel each other out. The historical Kennedy was a leader of grace and brilliance who inspired the nation to greater heights and a lazy, inattentive son of the leisure class who didn't do much. Snapper was a soul in tune and a magnificent slut.

As Pinky chuckled more about Lasky's lack of faith, Lasky continued watching the young man-woman and realized he had dreamed very recently about Snapper. But he could recall nothing more about it. Perhaps he dreamed of her often.

He remembered the first time he borrowed chips from her. He needed a bankroll fast to take on an easy mark who'd wandered into Bob's all the way from Argentina. The man was a bashful sort who stuttered from time to time. A purchasing manager from a department store looking for adventures to savor.

Lasky approached Snapper with trepidation, but she made the loan gladly. The Argentine turned out to be a cheerful loser, the sort who would be embarrassed if he somehow won. Lasky repaid Snapper that very night.

Later there were other instances when the outlook was less certain, the results less happy. He continued repaying her, but the bookkeeping became sloppy and a pattern developed, a gap between the sums of payouts and paybacks. Meanwhile, Snapper became plugged solidly into the crew at Bob's and was granted a measure of protection from all the misfortunes that could befall a call girl in Las Vegas.

Pinky's three ushers entered and poured their trays of bills, checks, and coins on a counting table. They were accompanied by Pinky's bodyguard and chief all-around flunky, Benny Blue Eyes. Benny wordlessly frisked each of the ushers as they exited one at a time. Obviously a routine procedure. Benny Blue Eyes was a body-builder with dark Puerto Rican features set off by a startling set of cruel blue eyes.

Pinky said, "What would you say? Medium?"

"Maybe better," said Benny, already counting.

"You know," Pinky told Lasky, "fund-raising is one of the least attractive aspects of this calling."

"I can see it breaks your heart."

Pinky told the young man-woman, "We wanna talk, Honey."

The honey put a tape of *Wheel of Fortune* on the VCR, turned up the sound, and returned to the pool table. Lasky understood it, but he still had trouble believing it—these people taped *Wheel of Fortune*. Pastor Pinky spotted the bandage on Lasky's hand, made a reflexive inquiry, then tuned out as Lasky gave him a quick explanation.

"I'm just here about our cigarettes, Pinky," Lasky said, changing course. As a sideline, Pinky sold cigarettes of dubious origin out of a warehouse near the airport. They were

12 to 15 percent cheaper than any other wholesaler's, and Tangeli would rather have his hair on fire than pay full price for anything.

"Christ, not again." Pinky yelled over at Benny. "Didn't I tell you to get that shipment out?"

"What shipment, boss?"

"The cigarettes for Bob's!"

"I musta forgot!"

"Well *un*forget! Today!"

"You got it!" the bodyguard said.

Lasky rose. "I'll count on that, then," he said.

"No, don't leave yet, Terry. Finish your drink. Let's talk some. You got yourself a good doctor for that hand?"

Lasky reseated himself but protested he couldn't stay long.

"Of course," Pinky said. "Shame about that armored-car job, isn't it?"

"Just awful," Lasky agreed.

Pinky gazed at Lasky with his little gray eyes that never lost their cheer. "Whoever's got that shipment now," he said, "man, they're riding one hell of a tiger. But you know, with the right partner, someone who's got the right connections, they'd get away clean. But like I said, they'd need the right partner." A vein in his surgically stretched forehead stood out more prominently now.

"Terry, I'm not going to insult your intelligence. I know you're a very intelligent man. An educated man. I know you know that those old dago mobs, they ain't what they used to be. But you got to understand, they're not powder puffs either. You can buck them, sure. But you need help. You need friends, Terry. We got only so much time we can move on this. Then it's . . .Money sitting around in cash like that, it's almost like a sin. We can put it into a numbered account, absolutely safe, and start earning interest. At least do that much.

"Look, ask anybody around this town if I ever screwed anyone on a deal. That's totally against what I believe, what we practice here. You do believe me, don't you?"

Lasky smiled and shook his head no. For a split second, Pastor Pinky lost his way then recovered.

"Damn, you almost got me," he said. "You're a funny feller, Terry. I mean that in a positive sense, of course. Course you believe me. You do, but a part of you is afraid to, afraid I'm . . .selling you snake oil, right? Look, Terry, everything'll be up front. My commission, everything. You just name the sum of the sandwich, and I'll tell you our end. But I don't think it'd cost you over 15, well, maybe 20 percent for the protection and security you're entitled to have.

"You need connections on this one. Connections and protection. We can give you everything, Terry. And hide you out while we get started. We got ourselves a network that the Mafia, the Costa Nostra, whatever they call themselves, they can't measure up with, believe me. But it's important we get started now.

"Look, I know about your service in Vietnam, the paratroops and everything. It still means something, sure. But not to those wop bastards, if you'll excuse the language. Sure, you're a tough man, but you're not tough enough to handle this yourself. Nobody is. They play different, Terry. They don't come at you man to man. But around here, we know how to watch each other's back. You throw in with us, and we'll ride it out together."

He paused for a response. Pastor Pinky was used to getting them. So Lasky shook his head no. Pinky plunged in again. The vein in his forehead throbbed.

"Look, Terry, I'm not even saying you can lay your hands on the money. But even if you can't, they think you can. Everybody does. That's where there's danger. Whether it's you or anybody else, whoever's got that cargo, if they were plugged into what I'm talking about, they could . . . I'm telling you they could . . . But you see, without the right connections, they'd be running scared the rest a their lives. Sneaking into their own money like burglars. If they live. But with the right partner, someone all hooked up to the right places, they could end up with hell, who knows? Double, their original haul. Maybe more than that. They could . . . They'd be too big for the mob to fuck with, if you'll excuse my language."

"Why tell me?" Lasky said.

"I'm telling it straight, Terry. I figure there's no better way to play it with you. Am I right?"

He waited for a response again. This time Lasky didn't give him any. "When that Berkeley whispered in your ear," Pinky said, "I don't figure he was whistling Dixie. I've handled deals like this before, Terry. I can't give you details because they're confidential. But I was made for this deal. We both were."

A buzzer went off, and the young man-woman crossed over to Pinky's desk to answer the intercom. A brief, inaudible conversation transpired.

Lasky got up. "I'll count on those cigarettes, then," he said.

"You've got to learn to trust, Terry. I don't mean to be critical, but—"

"Of course not," Lasky said.

The young man-woman, off the intercom now, tried to whisper in Pinky's ear. But the volume was still turned up on the VCR. On the screen, Vanna White pointed grandly to a necklace on display. "Dammit, I can't hear a thing," Pinky said. "Where the hell's the remote?" he said, searching. The young man-woman quickly turned off the TV, then returned to Pinky and tried to whisper again. Pinky screwed up his face. "Not now, goddammit!" Then he called out in a soft pleading voice to Lasky, who was headed toward the door. "Wait up, Terry."

"I'll be seeing you, Pinky," Lasky said.

"Be smart, Terry. You can trust me. And you need me, Terry. Ah, Terry—"

# CHAPTER TWELVE

# Snapper

Lasky was confused when he got out of the taxi. For one thing, three figures covered in black cloth bags stood like sentinels next to his Chinese neighbor's trailer. But the main problem was Lasky's trailer. It wasn't where it was supposed to be.

He looked around wildly. It was nowhere around, and no, he wasn't lost. Damn! He scrambled forward and tripped on the curb, bruising his toes. He kicked a discarded oil can, and it sloshed some residue back on his trousers.

His utility wires were cut, the pipes open and raw. Everything he owned was gone, snatched like a flimsy nest. Clothes, shoes, photos, music, all life's mementoes. He approached the three shrouded figures. "Where's my trailer?" he shouted. They stood silent, unmoving. "Have you seen my trailer?"

With his good hand, he grabbed one of them where the lapels ought to be. "Who the hell are you?" Lasky shouted.

He felt he might have seen these three before. He couldn't place where.

Lasky heard a voice call from a distance, "Hey buddy, was that your trailer?"

But he concentrated so hard on the three mysterious figures, he didn't decode the words off in the distance. "I said who the hell are you?" Lasky demanded, shaking the person in the black bag. Who offered no resistance. It was like shaking a doll.

"We're contemporary madness," one of the other figures answered finally. "The anonymity of pointless existence. Being and nothingness."

"Get it? Conceptual art, man," said the figure in Lasky's grasp.

Lasky released the person, evidently a man. "Are you crazy?" Lasky said.

"He gets it," said the figure who spoke first.

Said the third figure, "Our relative sanity has no more meaning than the absurdity of this or anything else in a dead, uncaring universe."

"We've reached you, right?" said the figure who spoke first. "I can see it." The figure produced a large, gaily decorated donation can that said "Yes" in bold letters. "And we welcome—"

"I don't fucking believe it!" Lasky said. He wished he was angry enough to kill them. Instead, he was only angry enough to suffer.

Lasky recalled reading about a European man—he couldn't remember in which city—who'd moved all his belongings into a new apartment, went out for a bite, and later discovered he left behind the address to his new home. All his possessions remained hidden somewhere in the cold, look-alike city streets that mocked his desperate, futile search.

"Hey buddy, was that your trailer?" a voice said again. This time it registered.

Lasky looked up and saw a woman sitting incongruously at a card table about forty yards away. She was set up next to Ike and Mike's traveling soup kitchen. "Was that your trailer?" she shouted again.

Lasky started toward her.

"Another stiff. This just isn't working, Harold," one of the three bagged figures said.

"What do you know about it?" Lasky shouted.

"They drove it away," the woman said.

"They? Who's they?"

"I dunno. They hitched it to a big semi and headed east, that way," she pointed. "They were wearing uniforms."

"Uniforms? What kind of uniforms?" Lasky pleaded.

"Blue, you know those things that they . . . Whaddaya call them? Blue coveralls."

Blue coveralls. Of course. Men in matching blue coveralls could do anything they wanted. They could carry the Mona Lisa right out of the Louvre, and the guards would hold the door open. These people were smart. He saw that now. Maybe too smart for him.

The woman who'd seen the men in blue coveralls wore a green armband, a man's hat, and a rumpled, itchy-looking suit too heavy for the heat.

She thrust a flier into the hand of a grandfatherly man tugging a toddler. They were just leaving the soup kitchen, and the old man had the appearance of someone who looks eternally as though he just lost his wallet. She handed a second flier to Lasky.

"You seen one a these?" she said. "Laura Lasky's speaking tonight. Come on down to Bob's."

Years ago Lasky left his address book behind on a plane. Frantic phone calls yielded nothing. Took him days to get over it. How does that compare to losing everything? He would need a new place to stay. But he didn't want to think about that now because he was already worrying about how much tighter Bitsy might turn the screws.

Absently, he read his flier: "Tired of politics?" it began. Followed by a hyped, three-paragraph biography of Laura and signed Solutions America. The talk was set for 8 p.m. in the Winchester Room of Bob's Beer and Guns. The room had been a ballroom years ago. Tangeli rented it out occasionally for special events.

Someone roughly shoved him from behind. He turned to face an angry Reverend Mike. "Hey, end of the line or you're outa here," yelled the feisty little man. Lasky, in his bewilderment, had stepped into the middle of a food line about twenty souls long. "Go on, get to the end," the minister said. "We got asparagus vinaigrette, salmon soufflé, and a chocolate mousse with raspberries and cream."

Lasky grimaced in additional anguish, then stepped away. The hooded figures waited, exuding hope and craziness, two emotions which perhaps belonged together. He went back and pounded on the door of his Chinese neighbor, hoping for information, but there was no answer. Once more he asked himself why, if the cargo were so dangerous, did everyone want it so badly?

❦

In a relatively quiet corner of Bob's, Snapper nibbled at a bowl of popcorn and savored the last several pages of *The Stranger*. In a recent Great Books discussion, her team leader had insisted the novel was Camus's portrayal of the certain disaster that must befall an absolutely truthful man, a man who would dare to tell the world he was unmoved by the death of his mother. An interesting interpretation. But rereading it, she still disagreed.

Once more she saw the revelations of a central character who did not understand he was alive until he had to die. An age-old theme, of course, but presented exquisitely in the original French, like a prose Renoir. Such a language helped Camus to see forever into the slow-motion, dream-like state of this life. These were concepts which could barely find utterance in Malay, a language for coconut gatherers who saw no reason even to specify verb tense or conjugation. How many Malays had seen their thoughts trampled in the womb because there was no way to express them?

But in America, even as an unheralded dark age descended over so much of its culture and economy, Americans astounded her with their resourcefulness and cheer. Her johns were always optimists. Like the western pioneers, they had hopes about what lay over the next hill. She loved the liars best of all. The fake arbitrageurs and airline pilots and espresso tycoons. There were times she felt she lived on the set of a Fellini film. It seemed only whores lacked the imagination to reinvent themselves.

Orientals, Snapper decided, were resourceful in less endearing ways. Clever but not wise. Like the Ngs, her mother's family. A cluster of calculating aunts, uncles, and cousins who chirped and argued and rushed about, laboring ceaselessly to form and feed a complicated jungle of interlocking businesses that enabled them to buy shiny mountains of things—gold watches, designer shoes and pens and luggage, Mercedeses loaded with tencho-gadgets. They feared and despised any free time, which made them nervous and deprived them of their work.

The Ngs were also fierce gamblers. More than once her grandfather placed great portions of his empire of tea plantations, rubber trees, and computer-chip factories at the mercy of a pai gow tile. On the last flip of the tile, when he lost everything, he realized time at last held value, for there was no more time to earn everything back. He jumped in front of a beer truck and died in the road like a snake.

Terry's gambling was of a different order. She could not discover its source. It did not drive him, and she could not sense it as part of his soul. But there were times it threatened to reduce his essence as a man.

Terry knew instinctively that people need not surrender their lives to the meaningless tedium that governs most of them most of the time. They say you can't run away from your troubles, he once told her. "But I've run from trouble lots of times when it worked out just fine."

There he was talking to Bob Tangeli at the bar. He did not look like a man who had just lost everything. No, he would never throw himself in front of a beer truck over the loss of something that could be purchased in a store. But he needed guidance nonetheless. Before they murdered him over nothing.

She was there in her corner, just as Lasky had hoped. Reading something. Hair shining, tied back in a simple ponytail that should have trailed down to the small of her back like a map of Chile. Instead it ended just below the neck, giving her a perter beauty. Long tantalizing fingers curled around the book. She looked like a princess with an Oxford degree and a full dance card.

Before he could approach, Lasky was waylaid by a baleful toad of a man in worn blue shoes and a spotted white suit who congratulated him for winning a complete Freudian analysis at no cost, starting immediately.

"Why me?"

Because, the man explained, Lasky fit some complex demographic profile his "institution" needed in order to complete a vital study. "I've been looking everywhere for you," the man said.

"You mean I can tell you all my secrets?" Lasky said.

"Of course."

"Piss off," Lasky told him, moving on. But he thought of something and doubled back to ask the Freudian, "Just because you're paranoid, that doesn't mean they're not out to get you, right?"

"That's not the way it goes," the Freudian answered. "Just because they're out to get you, it doesn't mean you're not paranoid."

"Thanks." Lasky saw Tangeli beckoning him.

"Been home yet?" Tangeli said.

"You heard, then."

Tangeli shook his head to show the futility of even commenting on the fickle jabs of Nature. "Where you been sticking that hand?" he said.

"I appreciate your concern," Lasky said. "It's just cut and

sprained. What's this?" he said, thrusting Laura's flier at him.

"It'll bring in business," Tangeli contended.

"In other words, she's not paying you anything," Lasky said.

"Hey, when Caesars gets a heavyweight fight, it makes money off the tables, not the gate."

"Laura Lasky's going to bring in a crowd of heavy hitters? Don't hold your breath." Without giving Tangeli a chance to reply, he headed straight for Snapper.

"See? They haven't killed me yet," he told her.

She continued reading.

"But they stole all my underwear," he said. Still no response. "They did, honest." He paused. "I was a jerk. I know it." He popped a couple popcorn kernels in his mouth. "May I?"

Snapper carefully placed a bookmark in her book, closed it, and looked up at Lasky. She rose, her expression serious, and embraced him. They kissed tenderly.

"That was vicious, stealing all your underwear," Snapper said as he held her. She gently caressed his bandaged hand.

"The fiends," he said, kissing her harder. They watched each other's eyes. "They took everything I own," he said, "except my wallet, keys and a cheap ballpoint. And the keys don't fit anything but a dead car and a missing trailer."

"But you also have a gun in your pocket—"

"I'm just glad to see you."

"And whatever was in that armored car," she said.

"That again?"

She didn't even ask about his hand. She knew everything about the attack at the projects, the missing trailer. By this time Lasky was a walking-around folk tale. There was widespread speculation on what they'd take next. A relative? A finger? Perhaps an ear.

Snapper stepped back. Looking at Lasky, she hugged herself. She wore a sleeveless shift, a garment that could not be worn in Malaysia, where women did not bare their arms in public. Just the feel of her own slender brown arms about her body made her feel sexy. She threw herself back at him and kissed him again as though he were going away.

# CHAPTER THIRTEEN

# Mussolini's Trains

Bags, who'd arrived very early, had a front-row seat inside Bob's ballroom, a musty ghost-town kind of space. It was packed with people as it must have been in the old days when there were hotel rooms on the property. Clouds of cigarette smoke swirled thick and choking in the glare of ancient overhead bulbs recessed within the once-ornate high ceilings. Folding chairs were running out fast. Bags figured there must be eight hundred people here. Amazingly, Laura Lasky's celebrity status was still breathing.

He would have bet she couldn't draw a minyan in this town. Perhaps it was still possible to forge a broad coalition around intelligent ideas. True, a couple oddballs with signs were outside protesting her once-despised blood drive for North Vietnam. But significantly, they had no organizational backers. Even the VFW was tired of Vietnam.

Extra waiters and waitresses worked the room in organized frenzy. Tangeli would make a killing on drinks and afterward suck some of this crowd over to his tables. No dummy, Tangeli.

The aging air conditioning couldn't keep up with all the bodies, and the air was hot and close. Bags would never get used to the city's grotesque Southwestern temperatures nor the harsh, angular shadows which seemed to protrude even indoors, like the stinging red ants. Nights like these were a preface to the relentless sunlight that would come the next day and the next, turning the air white and peeling the paint off fences the moment it was slapped on. Everything seemed poised to remind him he was a million light-years from the woodsy, snowy East he should have appreciated more when it was his.

Waiting for something to happen, Bags reflexively watched the flat opiate of a TV up high on the wall. Tuned to one of the sports channels, it showed a series of slalom racers. The TV helped him keep his eyes off Laura, sitting alongside her Fetherling. She'd already caught Bags searching the seductive spaces between the buttons of her navy-blue silk blouse in a fruitless effort to glimpse one of those perky red nipples.

Even when he was an Ivy League success, Bags was terrified of women like Laura. They transformed him into a pathetic, desexed glob. A Gabby Hayes eunuch who provided comic relief while John Wayne idiots got the girl. He was glib only when it didn't count.

It amazed him that insipid jerks like Fetherling could accept their lovely booty so calmly. As if they had it coming. Bags had been afraid to approach even his landlady Myra, a Camel-smoking light-heavyweight with oak-tree ankles who thought she was an intellectual because she worked crossword puzzles. Mercifully, she'd made the first move after several weeks of his fumbling.

Myra had canceled her last appointment and was in the crowd somewhere with her beautician friends. A Kennedy worshiper longing for new saints, her mind was stuck in place like a stripped car.

As stragglers still streamed in, Fetherling, all prettied up in a tie and shined shoes, approached the mike. If only Bags weren't a running joke of a felon perhaps he could have delivered the introduction. He'd have done well, too. Crowds weren't what threw him.

"Turn off the damn TV!" someone yelled. And sure enough, now that everyone was quieting down, Bags could hear an announcer discussing ice patches on the slopes in Chile. A bartender climbed up and shut him off.

Bags was displeased to observe that Fetherling was a capable speaker. With the aplomb of Letterman, he opened with a politically correct joke about the president's fondness for junk food and segued nicely into Laura Lasky's Madison Miracle, although he was careful not to call it that and possibly tag her with an old Dukakis label.

"When she was a senator in the Wisconsin legislature," Fetherling said, "Laura Lasky wrote a bill that threw the greedheads out of the auto-insurance business and established a system that has already been copied by eleven other states." Bags knew that wasn't entirely true, but it was close enough.

Fetherling went on to detail his boss's accomplishments in health care and welfare reform, plus what a delight she was to work for, how she forged relentlessly ahead even as it got tougher and tougher to accomplish anything in America's stalled political process.

"Laura Lasky hasn't given up," he reminded his listeners. "As national director of Solutions America [he quickly read off the toll-free number], she is working day and night . . ." When finally he introduced the honorable Laura Lasky, Bags was already standing and applauding. Laura singled him out with a socko smile, looking directly at him with the kind of attention generally reserved for rock stars and $400-an-hour attorneys. He brushed a hand south to make absolutely sure his fly was shut.

Her smile faded as she stepped up to the mike. She acknowledged the applause and looked around with tender patience, as though memorizing every face in the crowd for some future reward. "Thank you, Roy," she said at last, and as the applause started up again, she repeated the phrase twice until there was quiet. Then she was silent again, peering about inquisitively, looking very much at home.

"I'm asking you," she said finally, "to play a long shot."

That night Lasky invited Snapper to dinner on the flowered terrace of Alma's, a little residence converted to an alfresco Mexican cafe. Alma, an attentive, chubby optimist in a bright apron, kept their wine glasses filled and stuffed them with a subtly seasoned *pollo con arroz*. At the next table, an hourglass brunette with an endearing hooknose and supertight, starched jeans sat with an equally composed male companion. They both had a soft, samba quality to them that perfectly matched the contraband flavor of their surroundings.

Alma's terrace held only six tables. There was also a bar with three stools which were rarely filled. Yet the bartender, Alma's son, always behaved as though he expected a svelte, aftertheater crowd to enter any second to order martinis and trade pithy comments. Resplendent in his magnificent Hawaiian shirt, he was in absolute control of his universe—glasses, limes, and olives all lined up like Mussolini's trains.

After Alma saw them to the door, Snapper drove Lasky to her place. As they got out of the car, he spotted a man carrying a trash bag on his shoulder and chased him down.

He was hairy and lanky and his eyes stared widely, but it was difficult to tell what expression they formed. "You're not him, are you?" Lasky finally said.

The man circled Lasky like a pony on a tether, staring at him. "Not who?" he said. "Or do you mean not him?"

"Not him," Lasky replied. To make sure, he fished in his pocket and handed him two dollars.

"Thanks, friend," the man said, melting back into the night.

"Was it the same one?" Snapper said.

"Definitely not," Lasky said.

He followed her through the entrance of what used to be Whistler's Bowling Emporium and into the dust-caked confusion that some farsighted entrepreneur was converting into lofts. Snapper's was already completed.

Her apartment, formerly the bowling-alley kitchen, was an immaculate refuge sprinkled with skylights and accented with bold colors that glowed like fireplace embers. Lasky inspected the adjoining studio for new creations and found another one of those still lifes that looked like Snapper's interpretation of broken gizmos and soup spills. It leaned against the wall in a corner jumbled with easels, bottles, and other artist paraphernalia. Snapper drew a distinction between where she lived and where she worked. Life was neat, work cluttered and without boundaries.

"You still don't like my paintings," she said, coming up behind him.

"I see more to like each time," he said.

"Bullshit. Come on, I'll pour you something." He followed her back to her living quarters.

"You still have time to hear your speech," Snapper teased him as she poured his Chardonnay.

"Shut up," he said.

She sat down next to him, resting her fingers on the inside of his thigh. Her *matsoli*. Her white man.

Laura raised her feisty, pretty fist, shaking it in affirmation as she rewarded her listeners with a gritty, determined smile.

"Now the Constitution, we know, didn't instruct us to have politicians who were bought and sold," she said. "Trouble is, the Constitution, that document we were all taught to revere, hasn't worked to prevent it. Not even the Founding Fathers could foresee what we have today—this cruel, dreary breakdown—the fractured health-care system, the shattered schools, the drugs on every corner, guns in every pocket, frightened elderly cowering behind every window shade."

Bags bellowed his approval with the others, loving her faith and her deception, shamelessly bobbing his head into position to catch another glimpse of that wondrous nipple.

"Meanwhile, it's business as usual inside the Beltway, which sends out rivers of deceit that are infecting so many vital areas of our lives.

"And the problem isn't with this personality or that one . . . none of that *crap* the media focus on. And it's not, as I've been hearing lately, the end of the Cold War, the disappearance of outside enemies to keep us together.

"If we had to name the one ingredient that's paralyzing

and killing our government, ripping the guts out of the economy and flattening so much of what's good about our country—you know what that ingredient is? I'll tell you in one word, and see if you disagree. Sleaze. Sleaze!" She paused and looked around for a brief wave of applause. It came. "The perfectly legal institutional sleaze that's insinuated itself into our system like a Lyme tick.

"We don't have leaders anymore. We have humanoid auction pieces. So-called politicians who put themselves up for bid, openly, because they have so manipulated our laws that their hired-gun status is all perfectly legal—the way things get done. And so naturally, the voters, shut out of the nuts and bolts of the process, no longer trust the motives of anyone in office or aspiring for office. It's assumed they are either already bought and sold or trying to close the deal.

"While those judges, the so-called judges and *justices*"— smirking, she drew the word out slowly, provoking laughter—"who interpret the rules for this perverted structure have themselves been purchased by the same corrupt system they are supposed to pass judgment on."

She charged on through another wave of applause, waving a finger in the air. "And when we try to straighten things out, when some of us get together and even manage to make a few halting steps toward reform, the newspapers and networks—what do they call us? Flakes. We are *flakes*." She shook her head slowly like a tough mom protecting the cookie jar. "They laugh at us. Their automatic reaction toward anything approximating a noble cause. Because that is their part, their role in the theft of our hopes. If it's good, cut it down. Attack it. Improve the system? Impossible! Can't be done. They're dreamers, nut cases, don't take them seriously.

"So while we try to find out what is wrong and try to fix

it—the reporters, the journalists—what are they doing? Why they're all camped outside someone's boudoir trying to figure out who's sleeping with whom." Cheers and applause.

"And don't forget that a generous portion of the loot taken by these politicians of ours is paid right back to the media in the form of election advertising. It's an essential ingredient of the whole sorry system. The looters make sure only those with loot can score more loot. Everyone else is cut out of the circle. They're all flakes, remember? Flakes. Can't buy enough TV spots? Must be a flake.

"Well let me tell you something. The old media, they're on their way out now. Tom Brokaw and Barbara Walters may live in palaces and drive designer autos, but you can quote me, they're getting their . . .behinds . . ." She paused for a laugh. It came. " . . .whipped by the new cable channels and weekly shoppers and just tons and tons of new communications we can call cyberspace transmissions for lack of a better term. And poor old Tom and Barbara are so rattled by this competition that they're down in the dirt every day competing with the Geraldos and the *National Enquirer*.

"They don't even examine the system, much less make any sense out of it. Do you want to know how government works these days? Let me tell you. It's really quite simple. There's this big restaurant, and the service stinks, and the waiters are snooty, and the food is cold, and you wait hours for a table. And you know what it charges? Billions and billions of dollars. The name of this restaurant is Chez Government. And you know what else? We're picking up the check. You and me. But when our silverware is dirty or the steak is overdone or the eggs are runny, Chez Government doesn't care. Want to know why?"

"Why?" shouted hundreds of voices, Bags's included.

"Because we're just the suckers who pay the check. But they're jumping through hoops to earn a tip. Want to know who leaves that tip?"

"Yes!" shouted Bags. Laura gave him a swift, sweet glance which told him, Shut up, stupid.

"It's Westinghouse, General Electric, IBM, Donald Trump, Bill Gates, every plugged-in, in-the-know fat cat you can name. And compared to what we're paying and what that tip is costing us in terms of good government, it's one hell of a scrawny tip. Remember Keating? The so-called financier? If you look at what he paid out in tips—in, excuse me, campaign contributions—it's small change compared to what they let him steal from you and me, our parents, from our children yet to be born.

"And you know what? I don't think we have to take it anymore. What about you?" Shouts, applause— "Don't you want to put a stop to it?" More shouts and applause—

❧

Lasky wondered how she could possibly love this as much as he did. Yet it appeared she did. She was so shameless and sweet, submissive and assertive by turns, her eyes wide with soaring pleasure, anticipation, then near-closing in husky fulfillment. No hint of Judeo-Christian shame from Snapper. He drank in her languorous, long, perfumed limbs and understood, as always when he made love to her, that his dreamy luck knew no bounds.

Later she got out of bed, put on a kimono, came back, and snuggled up to him under the sheets. Always a bit shy about her body afterward. And quiet as their souls slowly separated again and they lay side by side, wondering about each other.

❧

He was a little guy in a wrinkled suit who walked like Frankenstein's little brother, arms stuck out in front and a little to the side. The arms didn't go back and forth at all, just hung there like penguin flaps. Tangeli knew he was trouble coming in the door even before he spotted Grinder, the Dentist, and several uniformed cops follow him in.

The little man waddled straight past a dumfounded Cap to the crap table and called a halt. Just like that, in the middle of a game, table full of customers left over from the Lasky broad's speech. They howled ready to kill, but the little man paid them absolutely no heed. He grabbed some dice, placed them in a micrometer gadget, then shook his head. He repeated the process at the other crap table.

He immediately advanced, arms inert, to a blackjack table. He halted that game, too, and started sorting the cards.

It was tough going, but Tangeli managed to maneuver his chair through the crowd. "I'll be with you in a minute," the little man said. Tangeli waited quietly.

"What we've got so far, Mr. Tangeli," he finally said, "are shaved dice on both the crap tables. Plus this blackjack shoe contains two extra fives. I think we both know why." The little man spoke with a New York accent and just a trace of a stutter.

"That's bullshit, and you know it," Tangeli said. "Somebody tampered with this stuff."

"Exactly," the little man said, stammering hard on that

one. Then he glared off toward the gun counter. "My God, you're selling guns."

"Don't tell me, let me guess," Tangeli said. "You're shocked, *shocked* to discover there's a gun counter in here."

The little man looked at him curiously, not getting the joke.

Tangeli addressed Grinder, who, as usual, looked both flustered and amused. "Where did you find the little schmuck?"

"Please leave my undersized dong out of this discussion," Grinder said.

"The other one," Tangeli said.

Ignoring the remark, the little man waddled over to another table. He created a screaming horde of angry players everywhere he went. The winners were angry because he broke up their streak, the losers because everything made losers angry.

"The other little schmuck is Mr. Kaye from the gaming commission," Grinder said, "and I guess you know you're being closed down."

It took hours for all the customers to cash their chips at the cage. But they all waited, fuming, because they feared tomorrow the chips would be worthless. It was like a run on a bank. Meanwhile, the little man called in assistants who videotaped proceedings, and somebody called in all the local TV crews, who taped every raging nutso they could find. And they found bunches. Everyone knew that cameras weren't allowed in casinos, but, of course, the cops wouldn't let Tangeli throw the media out. He tried calling everyone he knew with juice, but no one seemed to be in.

❀

Grinder took a breather outside. The Dentist followed. "I'll go you double or nothing on the Mickey game," Grinder said.

"Mickey Mouse," Joe shot back.

"Mickey Mantle," Grinder said.

Patrons were still streaming out like excited insects. They all talked a mile a minute, and Grinder heard one word over and over—"cheat."

"Mickey Finn," Joe said.

"Mickey Spillane."

"Mickey Rooney," Joe said.

"Mickey Cohen," Grinder said.

"Huh?"

"Gangster. Nineteen forties. L.A.," Grinder said.

"You been studying," Joe said. "Mickey the Monkee."

"What?"

"You know. "Hey, hey, we're the Monkees . . ."" Joe said it in cadence, almost actually singing. He didn't like to lose.

"Yeah, but Mickey what?" Grinder said.

"Mickey the goddamn TV Monkee," Joe said.

"All right. Mickey the Monkee," Grinder said finally. "But if you can't name him and I can, then I advance, too. Agreed?"

Joe gave Grinder just a hint of The Stare, then remembered himself and backed off. "Okay," he said.

"Mickey Dolenz," Grinder said.

"Shit," Joe said, clearly out of Mickeys.

Grinder watched Stalisi strut around the parking lot like a ninja rooster. He probably hadn't heard the conversation, but Joe breathed heavier, all at once angry. He didn't like anyone to see him take second. "You know," he said, "if this don't work, we'll hafta grab that cunt a his, like Stalisi says."

"Stalisi says. He says a lot of things," Grinder said. "But when he's through running off his mouth, he'll go back to Chicago, and we'll be here with the problems."

"No problem hiring a hooker and asking her for extras," Joe said.

"Listen, Joe, I worked for Bitsy before you ever heard of him. I know what works and doesn't work in this town. I get him what he wants, but I keep things balanced. He's smart enough to appreciate that. It's better for him, better for us. He wants wet work on this, well we're not part of that, because you start kidnapping people, everything's outa whack, understand?"

"Kidnapping? What're you talking?" Joe said. "I'm talking hiring us a bitch for a while, that's all. Anybody can hire a bitch. This Jew, he's pulling too much shit, Grinder. Stalisi's right."

"Stalisi again. Stalisi's not your partner; he's not your lieutenant either."

"Lieutenant my ass," Joe said.

"What did you say, detective?"

"Don't start that shit, Grinder. I'm telling you, I watch how things work around here, and it's not always like you say. Bitsy, he don't care how we do it, long as we don't tell him about it and long as the job gets done."

"It's not 'he don't care.' It's 'he doesn't care,' you dumb fuck. And of course he doesn't care. That's what I'm trying to tell you. Because you go blasting somebody, we're the ones stuck with the heat, not Bitsy. We've already got Feds nosing around."

"The Feds can't find their shoes in the morning."

"Sometimes they get lucky," Grinder said.

"What are you? Queer on this Jew or something?"

"Go make nice to your wiseguy, you dumb fuck," Grinder said.

"You always talk about Bitsy like he's the big boss. You still ain't figured out the real bosses're back east. So who's the dumb fuck? Bitsy's a fucking clerk, is what he is."

"Look," Grinder said, "out here he's the man. You know why? Cause the guineas don't trust each other. But they trust him. Get it, asshole? They can't trust each other. That should tell you something. Now this hijacking shit, it's giving us a high profile, understand? We have to think before we act."

"Call me that again and . . ."

"Call you what?" Joe said. "A dumb fuck or an asshole?"

Joe smiled. Grinder had seen this particular smile on him before, and he didn't like it. "Just don't call me dumb again," Joe said.

He didn't.

# CHAPTER FOURTEEN

# Blessing The Rastas

Because bars and casinos never close in Las Vegas, the padlocked Bob's Beer and Guns was an incongruous entity the next morning, almost like a corpse in a wedding party. Tangeli sat alone at the gun counter, alive with nervous energy, his mind flitting from one thought to another like a remote control zipping through channels. As he grew older, his dreams and memories merged more and more.

Tangeli was fifteen when Tank Flaherty laid it out for him back in Chicago. Tank stood like always outside the drugstore like a 260-pound, double-deck hydrant. "The kid signals the turnkey he needs to use the toilet," Tank explained. "Turnkey hits a buzzer and opens the bars. The kid doesn't know it, but he'd be better off just shitting on a blanket in his cell. Because then one a the big niggers in the same row, he gives the signal, too. Turnkeys, they're not supposed to let two out at a time, but they want to keep the big nigger happy 'cause he's the biggest, nastiest nigger in there."

Tank always, always smiled. The smile complemented the neatness of his appearance. Several years older than Tangeli, he was happy to interpret the world to him in parables.

"The kid's walking down the row, and next thing he knows, there's a blanket over his head. Nigger drags him in his cell, and the turnkey, suddenly he can't hear a thing. He buzzes the bars locked. Now the kid's got two choices. Eat the meat or take it in the ass. Happens in County every night, Bob."

Bob Tangeli never questioned the reliability of Tank's information. Lying wasn't part of Tank's makeup. When others questioned his veracity, they were liable to get slapped across an ear. Tank had a fuse. And for some reason Tangeli never understood, Tank carried a little twenty-two under his dark raincoat. As though there were somebody or something out there even he couldn't handle with his rump-roast fists.

Tangeli popped another beer from behind the bar. They didn't seem to be affecting him much. Even now, he visualized the rows of jail bars, the institutional disinfectant stink, the darkness, the pitiless turnkey. He could feel the scratchy fibers of the brown wooly blanket around his ears just as he imagined it then, when he gradually turned away from his petty burglaries and scams, the explosive street fights and spur-of-the-moment snatches. First he just became more careful, but eventually he found himself on a straight road, as though his feet just took him there.

Graduated from high school, he went to work at U.S. Steel, and enrolled in night junior college. He stopped coming around the pool hall, and when cashiers made a mistake in his favor, he returned the change.

Then one night smiling Tank Flaherty stole a car, drove to the lake, stuck the twenty-two in his mouth, and fired. Only then did Tangeli understand that the kid in the story was not just some generic victim without a face.

Meanwhile, Tangeli, no longer a member of the petty criminal underclass, was judged fit for military service, drafted, and sent to Vietnam, where one steamy night a Vietcong soldier took away life as he knew it. Inmate or soldier. It didn't seem to matter. No happy endings waited for him. He took a dispirited pull at his beer.

"Bob, we bring you somet'ing, mon!" someone shouted. Cap opened the door to the Rasta musicians. "We bring you somet'ing. Fine herb, mon. Here." The keyboardist handed him a fat brown Rastafarian joint. Tangeli took a strong pull and held the smoke down in his lungs, reliving an old sweet sensation. "Bless you," he told the Rastas, exhaling.

One by one, other employees and some of the regular customers stole back inside, toking on the Rastas' sacred weed, swapping stories of what they'd seen and heard. Last night was an instant fable. Martha brought doughnuts. Finally Lasky showed up.

"I guess maybe Bitsy sent us another message," Tangeli told him, briefly describing last night's raid.

Lasky looked like a kid whose bike was stolen. "It wasn't your fault," Tangeli said finally. "You had no choice, and maybe they didn't either. We should a figured this. They can't afford to look stupid."

Lasky said, "It was probably that little prick Chicago sent. Stalisi."

"They wouldn't make a move like this without Bitsy's okay," Tangeli said.

He passed his joint over to Lasky.

Cap approached. "You weren't here last night?" he asked Lasky.

Lasky shook his head no.

"Your wife, she gave—"

"Ex-wife," Lasky corrected him.

"Ex-wife," Cap said. "She gave a hell of a speech. Didn't you think so, Bags?"

"Hell of a speech," Bags said.

"You know, being closed down isn't so bad," Bob said. "It's the thought of those fucking lawyers that makes me sick. Either I lie down for this shit or I have to start with the lawyers. Probably years of lawyers. Right now I don't know what's worse."

"Lawyers are worse," Lasky said. "But maybe we can fix it without them. Looks like it's time to get everything settled anyway. I'll let you know how it turns out." He started for the door.

"Wait a minute," Tangeli told Lasky. "Cap, would you do me a favor? Go with him. It might put you in the middle of this. But what the hell. You're still on the payroll, right? Take it easy, though. Forget what they say. Just watch out for what they do."

"Don't be insulting me with payroll talk," Cap said evenly. "I didn't just work here for the payroll."

"Sorry," Tangeli said. "I'm not myself." Bob's Beer and Guns had long since become a shrine to Cap's newfound self, a ladder to dignity from his cardboard-box bedroom.

"They don't have any a those snakes, do they?" Cap said. "I don't mind dagos so much, but those snakes . . ."

"How you tell the difference?" the Rasta keyboardist said.

"All right, all right," Tangeli said. He knew they were trying to cheer him up, but he felt awfully old this morning. His advice to Terry had probably been bad. Now he was out of advice. He was no Tank Flaherty.

Bags pulled Lasky aside. "Before you go anywhere," he said, "I think we better talk."

# CHAPTER FIFTEEN

# New Deal

The four no-nonsense security guards who escorted Lasky and Cap into the eye-in-the-sky room stayed close as a bridal train until Bitsy dismissed them, which he did immediately. The old man sat watching the monitors, Stalisi on one side, Grinder on the other. The guards' departure might have cleared the tension had it not been for the added presence of Joe the Dentist, who stood at parade rest like Goliath waiting to smite any Hebrew stragglers. Lasky saw no spotters or technicians about. The room was cleared for business.

Bitsy didn't bother to introduce himself. His spotted face and lanky form were famous around Las Vegas, which had always paid homage to men like him. "This is my favorite spot in the whole world," he said, eyes on the monitors. "Not down there with all the noise and yelling. Up here, where I can quietly watch the suckers grind themselves into little pieces. It's aces wired, fellas. Aces wired."

He gave Lasky the impression he knew what was going

on in this room without needing to look at it. Like a poker player who could name everyone's hand down to the last card. "Sit down, sit down," he said.

Lasky found himself looking to Cap, who didn't move. "You shouldn't a fucked Bob Tangeli like that," Cap said evenly. He addressed Bitsy on an equal footing, shattering the carefully constructed atmosphere of dominance. "He never did a damn thing to you."

"Yeah?" the Dentist said. His eyes turned instantly round and crazy.

"Who are you?" Bitsy said.

"Cap. I work at Bob's."

"Everything goes okay, this Tangeli, he'll open up again," Bitsy said. "He's just had a touch of lousy luck, is all. We're dealing with serious business here, so we had to get serious."

He turned to look at Lasky, and his voice turned hard. "On account a you," he said. "On account a your stubbornness. Everybody who knows me, they know I don't like to use muscle. But let me tell you—" He looked at Lasky like he was a troublesome car "—I don't consider you such a precious resource. I've seen plenty a guys like you. You're not so unique."

Lasky looked straight at a spot on Bitsy's spotted forehead just above the bridge of his nose. An interview trick to make Bitsy believe he was unafraid to look into his eyes. But he probably wasn't fooled.

"Maybe it's time to forget the bullshit and make a deal," Lasky said.

"No more bullshit's right," Bitsy answered. "And the deal's the same." He got up and moved toward the elevator. "I'm going to play some handball, take a shower. You guys set everything up." He glowered at Lasky. "But like you said, no more bullshit. 'Cause if there is any more bull-shit, I'll take it serious. As serious as I take anything." He addressed Grinder, "You know what I want."

"I need to see you alone first," Lasky said.

Bitsy thought it over just a second and nodded his okay.

"You'll have to stand for a frisk," Grinder said. Lasky handed him the pistol holstered in the small of his back. Grinder quickly patted him down anyway. Bitsy led Lasky into a smallish men's room across from the elevator.

"What is it?"

"Standard finder's fee is 20 percent," Lasky said. "Ask any insurance company. The total was three million, one hundred forty thousand. That leaves me six hundred twenty-eight thousand. Agreed?"

Bitsy burst into laughter—genuine laughter, but with a hard edge.

"I'd always heard you were an intelligent man," Lasky said, "so let's not play games."

"Ten," Bitsy barked. "Ten percent. And that's it. I ain't no rug merchant."

"Okay," Lasky said.

"You deliver the goods personally," Bitsy said.

"Agreed."

Bitsy opened the door and called in Stalisi.

"We're giving him ten percent," Bitsy told Stalisi.

"What?"

"We were stupid enough to lose it. He's right we should pay a penalty. I'll split the costs with your uncle."

Stalisi looked from Bitsy to Lasky and back again. "I'll call him," he said. He said it like it was a promise to murder both their families. Bitsy gave a hint of a sneer as he led the way out of the men's room. He whispered something to Grinder and disappeared down a staircase.

"C'mon," Grinder said, "let's get it done."

"I need to know everyone walks away," Lasky said.

"Bitsy never welshes," Grinder said. "You know that. You gotta learn to trust people."

"I've been told that," Lasky said.

Stalisi looked at his watch. "Twenty four hours," he said. "We need it back in twenty four hours."

"Why wait?" Lasky said. "Make it midnight."

They agreed. But then the Dentist approached Lasky like a downhill truck, stopping when he was nose-to-nose. "Remember. No more a your bullshit."

"I'm tired of this jail-yard crap," Lasky started to say. But Joe backhanded him before all the words got out. A backhand that snapped out like a switchblade, putting Lasky on his ass, palms behind him. The floor was blue tile. He hadn't noticed before. One side of his face felt numb, and his bandaged hand started aching again. The Dentist stood over him, and Lasky knew a kick might follow.

"Back off, Joe!" Grinder yelled.

"Your ape's out of control," Lasky said.

"I said back off, Joe," Grinder said.

The Dentist looked over at Cap, who watched noncommittally, as though in a theater. "What're you looking at, nigger?"

Cap smiled. "Your man's good with words," he said to Grinder. "Good with slaps, too. And I can understand your predicament. You don't want some candy-ass. You want good muscle to back you up. But good muscle, it can be kind a crazy, too. It's like breeding racehorses. They're looking for speed, but these other things show up because lots of times their mommy and daddy, they were brother and sister, or something. They get fast horses, but they're fucking stupid and crazy. Like I said, it's a predicament."

Now the Dentist smiled, too, breathing easy, and Lasky was even more conscious that Grinder had his pistol. Grinder clamped a hand on the Dentist's bicep. "You boys are making this a lot harder than it has to be," he said.

Lasky rose. "You know what? You'll have to throw in another forty thousand," he said.

"What?" Grinder said.

"You heard me. It's damages. You can explain to Bitsy that your endomorph here's responsible."

"You nuts?"

"Find him if you have to," Lasky said. "But that's the deal now. I don't like him ducking out and leaving the maniac off his leash. He hires him; he's responsible for what he does."

Grinder's eyes widened in appreciation. "You almost had me going," he said. "But no way."

"No deal, then."

"Bullshit," Grinder said.

"Only half bullshit," Lasky said. "Make it twenty, Grinder, or it all blows up in your face."

Grinder turned to Stalisi. "Give him another five so we can get outa here," he said.

"Sure, why not?" Stalisi replied, very cool now.

"Fifteen," Lasky said.

"Ten," Grinder said. "Period."

Lasky named his location. Grinder went along. "If we see any goons before then, anybody, anywhere, it's all off," Lasky said. "Don't follow me, you got that? You're getting off cheap, Grinder. Don't fuck it up. And give me back my piece."

"You won't need it," Grinder said.

"Then neither will you," Lasky said.

Grinder handed it to him. "There are a couple Feds," he

said. "Their names are Turnquist and Hernandez. They're about forty years old, and they look like Feds look. You know either of them?"

"I used to know Turnquist," Lasky said. "One of the dumbest cops who ever tried to bust a stolen-car ring."

"That's him," Grinder said. "He and Hernandez have been sniffing around this. If you happen to see them, they ain't with me, got it? You'll just have to handle them."

Bags was smiling as he stepped out the door of Denny's. This time, just for a change, he'd eaten lunch with his coffee. Not even the Bunsen burner air that hit him as the door opened could change his mood. Then he heard the question, "What's new, Professor?" And looked up to see Joe the Dentist.

Bags thought perhaps he should run. In fact, he knew he should run, which is what any two-bit felon with an ounce of sense would do. But Bags, even though he'd received a postgraduate education at Leavenworth, was a confirmed product of the Wasp middle class who couldn't bear to make a scene. The lanky behemoth with the cruel eyes led him into the car he had waiting.

Joe the Dentist started the engine. "Now just what was it you just told your little Fed pals?" he said.

## Chapter Sixteen

# Say Tennessee

Grinder lit another cigarette to mask the stench. This particular dump, a dozen miles from anything, had been closed for years now, so it was a subtle stink, but intrusive nonetheless. Lasky was smart to choose this place. Old garbage had a way of leveling things out.

Right on time a minivan came through the broken gate, the driver maneuvering carefully around ruts and clumps of smashed rubble in the road. Grinder reached inside the dash of Joe's car, blinking the headlights off, then back on. Lasky was at the wheel, the lanky black man next to him.

When he pulled to a stop, Lasky looked an awful lot like somebody trying hard not to look rattled. Grinder could almost feel sorry for him. He didn't ask for any of this. The cargo just landed in his lap like Michelle Pfeiffer licking his ear. Stalisi was too much of a putz to understand.

For a while Grinder thought there must be more to Stalisi than meets the eye. But finally he concluded no, there wasn't. There was nothing complex about Stalisi. He was such a common species of asshole, the Germans even had a word for it. *Radfahrer.* Someone who flatters superiors and browbeats subordinates. Grinder had basically seen him on only one end of the equation, but it didn't take much imagination to envision him sucking around his uncle's crotch like a Chihuahua. Now he was trying to stand around like he had a ramrod up his ass, but it didn't work. He was in a trash dump, and his eyes were glassy with fear and cocaine.

"Everything okay with the cargo?" Grinder said.

"We can only hope," Lasky replied.

"What is this? A waltz? C'mon, it stinks here. Let's do it."

"Joe the Dentist!" Lasky called out. "I didn't see you over there. How's Mrs. Dentist? All the little Dentists?"

The Dentist ignored him. Thank God for that.

"Can you keep still in there?" Pinky asked Benny Blue Eyes again.

"Why? Djoo hear anything?" his bodyguard answered from inside the closet.

"No, I . . .I guess it's okay," Pinky answered. "Sure you can see all right?"

"No problem."

"Now remember, don't make a move till I say something about Tennessee. If I do, come out with both guns up. If I don't say it, then I haven't seen the money yet, and you just stay put. Got it?"

"I know, I know."

Pinky needed a drink. He began fixing one.

"What's going on?" Benny said.

"Goddammit, stay put and shut up. For all you know he coulda been in here. It's almost time."

"I woulda heard him come in."

"Please, please shut up," Pinky said.

"Okay," Benny said.

❧

"This is it. Park across the street," Laura Lasky said.

Roy did a clumsy U-turn to the opposite curb and tried to straighten the car out, but he was too nervous, and finally he just left the tail sticking out in the street.

"Do you want me to do it?" she said.

"Okay, okay," he said, trying again, backward and forward. He used the mirror to back up, not turning around. Roy was not the best driver even under normal circumstances.

"Turn it off," she said.

He let out a deep breath of frustration and switched off the ignition.

"Give me the keys, please," Laura said.

Even in the darkness, she could see the Temple of Worth was an incredibly grotesque building. The idiotic attempts at tropical landscaping only made everything worse. Like the rest of this vapid city, it had a tawdriness deep in the caked, ugly soil. Trying to tame the irresolute sand with chemical fertilizers and imported water was wretched quackery—a mindless and vulgar plastic surgery. Everything should have been left to the coyotes and rattlers.

"Laura, I'm getting really bad vibes," Roy said. "Really bad."

"You had bad vibes before I ran for mayor, remember?"

"Not like this," he said. "This is really stupid. Really, really stupid."

"I promise you it will be all right," she said. "When we get back, you can have Walter's office, okay? Don't worry, Terry won't let anything happen to me—us," she quickly corrected herself.

"He might not even know it's us coming in," Roy said. "The guy is . . .Face it, he's unstable. And just showing up like this . . .It's dangerous. We're relying on the word of a crook, a jailbird."

"Sure, but—"

"Something's wrong. I feel it. It . . .Why are you so certain Terry won't pull something?"

"Because he's crazy about my ankles," she said. "Come on. I know they're in there. Just let me do the talking. They should be dividing it up by now. If that door the professor described is closed, we'll know there's a problem, and that'll end it, okay?"

"We'll just leave?" he said hopefully.

She opened the door of the car—

"Freeze, freeze!" Someone drilled a gun barrel into her forehead. She looked toward Roy—"I said freeze, goddammit!" She froze.

Determined people with guns scrambled nervously all around her. They wore dark jackets with bright yellow letters on the back. She felt nausea as someone grabbed the keys from her hand. "This guy's packing heat!" a voice yelled from the passenger side. They had Roy splayed out on the ground and whimpering while somebody threw open the trunk.

Next thing she knew, someone tossed her on her belly and drove a tree stump of a knee deep between her shoulder blades. She struggled to protect her face against the asphalt. "Cuff her, cuff her, goddammit!"

"You're under arrest. You have the right to remain—"

"Hey, I know her. It's that commie bitch. You know—"

"Aw-*right!*"

※

"Jesus, there's a damn army out there!" Pinky yelled. "Benny, Benny! It's Tennessee, Tennessee—"

Benny came out blasting—

Pinky sank to his knees and covered his expensive face. "No, don't shoot me, goddammit!"

※

Someone yanked Laura to her feet as gunshots erupted all around her. "Who's firing? Who's shooting at us, goddamn you?" A round-faced man with startled eyes shook her by the arms as she tried to curl into nothing. The figures in dark jackets—there must be dozens—were all shooting at the building.

"Wait! Wait! Who gave the order to fire?"

The loathsome shooting went on as the terrible man let her go. Hands cuffed behind her, she threw herself back on the sweet Las Vegas asphalt and prayed for help. Her front teeth ached like death, and she felt blood in her mouth.

"Hold your fire! Hold your fire!" After what seemed like a very long, frazzled time, the shooting stopped, only to begin again, more intensely. Seconds later, it died out again. Someone was shouting instructions over a public-address system. It sounded like one of those awful squawk boxes outside a fast-food drive-up window.

"Don't shoot! Dear God, don't shoot!" she heard a voice yell from inside the building.

It was answered by more squawking from the public-address system. It hurt her teeth to move her head, but she looked up. After awhile she saw two figures stumble out of the building with their hands reaching toward the next galaxy. They were set upon by a busy swarm of shouting figures in dark jackets.

As more time passed, she began to believe that she might not be killed after all. By the time she arrived at the hospital with her chipped, loosened teeth, bruised and bleeding knees and pitiful, red-faced lover-assistant, she was beginning to reassert herself.

When she finally deduced from their robotic chatter and frightened faces that not one cent in loot had been found anywhere, she began daydreaming sweet lawsuit dreams. This might not be so bad after all, Professor McBannister. Thank you, wherever you are, you pitiful little convict with your silly remnant hairs combed and glued over your bald head. I may owe you one after all.

Laura realized she'd been praying back at the raid and that it made her feel better. What the hell, no one would know about it. She began praying again—this time pleading with God to please let her be here when they brought Terry Lasky in dead. Or maybe crippled. Crippled would be okay, too.

"You never said what was wrong with the old gas station," Lasky said. "Why'd you have me change it?"

"Wasn't safe," Grinder said.

"Yeah, but why wasn't it safe?"

Cap and the Dentist transferred two cartons from one vehicle to another. "That's all of it," Cap said. Lasky was very aware that no one had answered his question.

Joe the Dentist slammed the trunk and lit a cigarette, leaning against the car. "You know your professor friend was double-crossing you?" he said.

"What are you talking about?" Lasky said.

The Dentist laughed a humorless laugh. "You worried about him or something? I just told you he was trying to fuck all of us. He was squealing to the Feds. You understand squealing, sheenie. I know you do."

"You stupid cocksucker," Lasky said. "He was just throwing them off. He sent them over to Pinky's, you stupid sonofabitch. He got them out of the way."

"Whaddya know?" the Dentist said. "That's just what he told me."

Lasky heard something. He turned, saw movement, and using a two-handed grip, he emptied his pistol at a figure in the darkness as he heard a machine-gun burst. Diving to the ground, he fished clumsily for another clip. He could shoot okay, but reloading was slow with a gimpy hand.

Stalisi scrambled behind the Dentist's car. The Dentist fired. Cap fell. Shots came from everywhere, and the Dentist went down in a heap as Grinder fired what seemed like a dozen shots at his partner. Stalisi, crouched behind the fender, yanked on the trigger of a big semiautomatic pistol like a panicked recruit. Grinder screamed and fell as Lasky, finally reloaded, squeezed off four quick shots at Stalisi's handsome head. Stalisi tumbled backwards.

Keeping his pistol on the crumpled form of the Dentist, Lasky crept forward to check him out. There was an awful gurgling in the big man's throat, and his beard was soaked with blood. His eyeballs were moving around frantically, as though searching for something. Lasky leveled his pistol—

"No, no, no!" Grinder yelled. Lasky stopped. "Oh, the dirty motherfucker," Grinder moaned. "He knew I was wearing a vest so he shot me in the balls."

"You, too?" Lasky asked him.

"They got you in the balls, too?" Grinder said, puzzled.

"No, I mean I'm wearing a vest. You know, I noticed everybody looked a little too wide."

"Better stay down," Grinder said. "There's somebody out there with a machine gun."

"I think he's finished," Lasky said.

Something snatched Lasky's calf in a vise and dragged him down. It was Joe the Dentist, his Cossack face red as death, his eyes bulging with the fury of hell. Lasky shot him in the abdomen, but the Dentist just slapped the gun away. Lasky thumped his tormentor with his good fist. The Dentist threw himself on top and chopped a marble fist down on his face—once, twice.

A part of Lasky flirted with unconsciousness, but oddly, the new pain helped clear his head. He searched for a makeshift weapon on the ground with his good hand while the Dentist's sticky hands found his throat and squeezed hard.

Lasky, unable to breathe, searched for a rock or anything to strike or stab with. Coming up empty, he stuck his arms beneath the hulking body, working both hands under the Dentist's crotch, then shoved both thumbs into the scrotum, drilling them upward, just like he'd learned at Fort Benning. Nothing. No reaction. Must be a capon.

His thumbs twisted and pushed with a desperation all their own, but he was losing strength fast. Gunshots exploded, once, twice. The Dentist stiffened, then went limp.

Lasky gulped air hungrily. He scrambled up from beneath the Dentist's body.

"Had to reload," Grinder explained.

"Maybe we should drive a stake through his heart," Lasky said. His neck was stiff, the left side of his face felt like it had been tenderized with a hammer, and his bad hand was on fire. But all in all, he felt pretty good.

He stumbled over to Grinder. A thin fountain of blood was shooting from his thigh.

"Shit, look at that, will you?" Grinder said. "Why does everybody have to shoot at me?"

"You have that effect on people," Lasky said, working fast. "But they missed your balls entirely."

Lasky removed the shoe and sock from Grinder's injured leg, then tied the sock in a tourniquet just above the puncture. Immediately, the fountain stopped, and Grinder's color improved. Lasky stuck a spent magazine in the knot and tied a new knot over that, twisting. "Hold this," he instructed him. "But you can't leave it on more than ten minutes."

Next he checked out Cap, who was barely conscious but breathing and trying to groan.

"I'll be right back," Lasky told him. Staying low and careful, he came up behind the stranger with the submachine gun. It was one of those compact little numbers that gave erections to gun crazies. "This guy's dead!" he yelled toward Grinder. Lasky didn't recognize him.

"Don't touch anything!" Grinder shouted back.

Lasky ran back to Cap and helped him out of his flak vest. There was a purple bruise on his side that grew while you watched it. Cap's face formed a shocked smile, as though he'd just discovered a vein of diamonds. "You know? I think you're mostly okay," Lasky said. He asked Grinder, "Who was the guy with the machine gun?"

"He was news to me," Grinder said. "I'd guess he was some asshole Joe knew from somewhere. Hope he wasn't another cop."

"He didn't look like a cop," Lasky said, "but neither did the Dentist."

"You know," Grinder said, "a sharpshooter with a good rifle could have sat there and taken us real easy. But this riffraff nowadays, all they know is to automatic fire. We were lucky."

"Grinder, you shot your own partner," Lasky said. "I'm touched."

"He needed shooting," Grinder said. "And it seemed like a good time to do it. Can anyone trace your gun to you?"

"I bought it from a Marine in Saigon," Lasky said.

"Excellent," Grinder said. "Let me think now . . . You check Stalisi and get me the two-way radio sitting on the dash. Don't touch anything else."

Stalisi's face was a mass of blood, and his arms and legs were twisted in a way that indicated he was dead before he fell. Lasky brought over the radio.

"Dead," Lasky reported.

"Okay," Grinder said. "Wipe your gun down. It belongs to the guy with the machine gun, get it? He shot Stalisi. And Joe gets Stalisi's gun. He shot me. Watch that gauze on your hand. Don't lose any threads off it. Hurry up, willya? I'm bleeding here."

Lasky planted both guns. The back of the Dentist's head looked like Jack Kennedy's in the Zapruder film.

"Good," Grinder said. "What happened is, Stalisi got a tip to come out here on an insurance case, and we agreed to accompany him. Joe had this stooge planted out there. Joe went nuts, which is easy for anyone to believe, and he started shooting at me, so I shot back. And the guy out there, he shot Stalisi. You and . . . Whatsyourname?" he asked Cap.

"Mother Theresa," Cap said. His voice was shaking just a bit as he grew used to the idea he was alive.

"You and Mother Theresa weren't here."

"I'm beginning to like this cop," Cap said.

"But now the guy with the machine gun fired two guns—the pistol and the machine gun," Lasky said. "And Joe had two guns, too. Who'll buy that?"

"You kidding?" Grinder said. "People carry two guns just to buy groceries. Half the cops I know carry *three* guns. They make Ross Perot look like he isn't paranoid."

"All right," Lasky said. "But powder burns and—"

"Don't worry about all that bullshit," Grinder said. "I just need the right bullets to match the right guns. I can take care of everything else. It's my investigation. Now what about the money?"

"What about Bags?" Lasky said.

"If Joe says he wasted him, well, he wasted him. He'll probably turn up in a car trunk. I don't think he had time to bury him in the desert."

"Why couldn't we meet at the gas station?" Lasky said.

"Joe said an informant tipped him the Feds might show up," Grinder said.

"What I still don't understand, then," Lasky said, "is just who was in on the double cross?"

"Maybe just Joe," Grinder said. "But most likely Stalisi, too. Maybe Bitsy, too. Maybe all of them plus the uncle, Venassio. We might never know. You know, if it hadn't been for Mickey Dolenz, maybe Joe wouldn't have whacked out like this."

"Mickey Dolenz?"

"Too long to explain," Grinder said. "Anyway, far as I'm concerned, it was all of them. Now like I said, what about the money?"

"Guess there's more of it now," Lasky said. He pulled the cartons out of the Dentist's trunk and informed Grinder he could find the body of the second hijacker, the van, and eighteen thousand in cash in the basement of the abandoned postal warehouse.

"Look," Grinder said, "we have to move fast here. I want to get some help for my balls—"

"Your balls weren't touched," Lasky said.

"Whatever. Don't make me repeat myself. I'm into stealing, understand? I'm a crooked cop and the son of a crooked cop. It's a much-abused but necessary calling. So I want a piece of the action. The real action."

"You get Bags' share," Lasky said. "We'll count it all out and find you. Or you can take it now and hit the emergency room with a whole lot of bills in your pockets."

Lasky watched Grinder consider whether he could really trust him. "Okay," he said. "Catch me later. But I need to know my share now. And who to see."

"It'll be me or Tangeli," Lasky said. "There used to be five shares—three hundred fourteen thousand divided by five. But the pot just went up to three million, one hundred forty thousand minus the eighteen thousand you'll report found to make you look like a great detective. Now we divide by six. That's—"

"Five hundred twenty thousand, six hundred sixty-six dollars," Cap said.

"I think Mother Theresa's going to live," Grinder said. "But why six shares? Bags is dead, I get his share, right? Still five."

"You'll have to trust me on that, too," Lasky said. "There are six shares. And if Bags is alive—"

"He isn't," Grinder said.

"If he is, you may only get one-seventh instead," Lasky said. He asked Cap, "How much is that?"

"It's . . .less," he said.

"What're you going to tell Bitsy?" Lasky said.

"I don't have that part worked out yet," Grinder said. "I don't even know if he tried to screw us, or we're screwing him first. I'll probably just have to gamble that his teeth aren't sharp enough these days to waste a cop. Where you taking your share?"

"G. Gordon Liddy," Lasky said. "What did he say when he got out of the joint? East of the sun and west of the moon."

"You better disappear better than he did," Grinder said. "He's on the tube every other week."

Lasky decided it was a good time to ask the whereabouts of his trailer and earthly possessions.

"Forget it. Everything's picked clean," Grinder said. Lasky figured as much. "If it had been up to me," Grinder said, "they'd have let you keep your Barbie Doll collection."

"I think I'm going to miss you," Lasky said.

"You think?" Grinder said, insulted.

# CHAPTER SEVENTEEN

# Kala

"Remember, no matter what they say, they won't mean it. They'll still try to kill you," Tangeli told Lasky. "And you," he said to Cap, "you were with him when he made the deal."

"Has anybody even considered giving it back to the owners?" Snapper said. She wore a brisk gray dress and heels, looking beautiful and businesslike in her last-minute flight clothes. They sat in a Ramada Inn suite in San Diego, a couple miles from the airport, a pile of currency on the kitchenette table. They'd barely talked on the plane. Tangeli showed up in his van three hours after the others checked in.

"Okay, who's it belong to?" Lasky said.

"The government?" she said. Cap laughed.

"I mean if we give it to them, they could help us," she explained.

"Some of it belonged to the IRS," Tangeli said, "but if you told them about it, they'd take it all. Fact is, the wiseguys and their partners are the real owners. It's house money. But if you give it back to them, they'll just—"

"I know. They'll try to kill me anyway," Lasky said.

"Why not give it to the suckers who lost it at the tables?" Cap said. "We could put an ad in the paper."

"This is what we're going to do," Lasky said. "Equal shares, just like before, only now they're bigger, and now there are six."

"What do you figure?" Cap said. "You giving Bags' share to his girlfriend? They didn't even live together."

"She'll just tell somebody and get herself killed," Tangeli said. "We wouldn't be doing her any favors."

"One share to each of us," Lasky said, "plus one to Grinder. If Bags is found dead, or if he doesn't turn up in a week, Rabbi Ike and Reverend Mike get his share."

Cap and Tangeli burst into laughter. Snapper looked puzzled. "But aren't they crazy?" she said.

"Maybe," Lasky said.

"You're not some new religious Lasky, are you?" she said.

"No."

"Because if you weren't just a little rotten, you might stop being interesting."

"No problem. I can stay rotten. Easy. But Ike and Mike will bring us luck," he explained, an idea so preposterous everyone agreed to it immediately.

Tangeli said that if Bags had to be dead, he hoped he was in the desert somewhere. "He'll have good company out there." They toasted the professor with drinks from the little hotel refrigerator. It was widely believed that the desert around Las Vegas was amply sprinkled with the makeshift graves of dealers from the old days—dealers who'd tried hidden pockets, accomplices posing as lucky players, and all manner of other tricks to smuggle chips from mob tables. Enough bones had been found over the years to give the tales credibility.

The four of them went to work separating the bills into six equal stacks. Tangeli would distribute the shares to Grinder and either Bags or the traveling soup kitchen, however it turned out. It took them almost an hour to count out all the twenties and hundreds and double-check the sums.

"If nobody needs me for anything, I think I'll just scatter," Cap said, zipping up a gym bag filled with his share. "Nobody knows where anybody goes. Right?"

"You can look me up anytime," Tangeli said. "I'll be selling beer and guns out of the same joint. Just wait another forty years so nobody recognizes you."

"They'll recognize me," Cap said. "Cause I'll still be beautiful." He sank to his knees and hugged Tangeli, burying his face in his shoulder.

"Get outa here, you bum," Tangeli said in an anguished whisper. The others took turns shaking hands with Cap, who charged out the door into sunshine and uncertainty.

"Why won't you come with us?" Snapper asked Tangeli.

"I appreciate the offer, sweetheart, I really do," he said. "But gimps can't disappear so easy. My best chance is to stick it out in Vegas. If I do, they'll figure I didn't get a slice. You forget, I understand guineas from the inside out. The other thing is, I want to open up again, clear my name."

"Clear your name? What are you talking about?" Lasky said. "You're a thief."

"Maybe, but they said I was cheat."

"When you see Grinder," Lasky said, "tell him to watch out for you, okay? He won't mind."

"We'll watch out for each other," Tangeli said. "But there are no guarantees."

"You know," Lasky said, "if they don't waste you, you'll still end up in lawyer hell over your license."

"Nah, I'll just pay off the little prick from the commission," Tangeli said, patting his pile of bills. "And if I can't get to him, I'll find someone on up the line. I don't need any lawyers to show me around Vegas. Now beat it, okay?"

Lasky hesitated. "You don't need help with anything?"

"No, I'll leave my van here awhile and rent a car to go back. That way I can slink back into town without getting spotted."

"I'd like to tell you where we're going," Lasky said.

Tangeli shook his head no. They shook hands, a somber act among friends too familiar to exchange handshakes. Lasky was afraid Snapper would cry now, but instead she kissed Tangeli with a big smile like she expected him to live forever. Maybe he would.

"Bob really does belong in Las Vegas," Snapper said on the plane into San Francisco. They figured to catch an international flight from there.

"He even likes the weather," Lasky said. "Grinder's the same way. They'd rather take their chances with the mob than leave town."

"What are their chances?" Snapper said.

"They're figuring the wiseguys are weak, and that anyway they won't go after cops or cripples."

"But what are their chances?"

"I don't know," he said.

"Don't start feeling guilty," she said. "White men always want to feel guilty. Whatever happens, Bob would rather die than become l'etranger."

"The stranger," Lasky said.

"Very good," she said. "But also foreigner, outsider. French is a precise language, but to the French, a foreigner is always an outsider, a stranger. So it doesn't differentiate. It's just *l'etranger*. That's me. From now on, it'll be you, too."

"It suits me," he said.

"I think so, too."

She rested her hand lightly along the inside of his knee. He loved traveling with her. "What's your name?" he said. "Your real name."

"Kala. But don't bother to learn it. I'll think of another one before we land."

"Too bad. I like it."

"I'll let you name me if I can name you," she said.

"No deal. You did bring a passport," he said, suddenly remembering.

"What do you think? I came to America in a turnip truck?"

"More like a turnip boat," he said.

"Caesars Palace brought me over to Las Vegas on one of its private planes," she said. "I was with Ernie Chang. Ever hear of him?"

"Nope."

"For a wiseass, you don't know much do you?" she said, squeezing his knee.

"Nope."

"He owns half of Singapore," she said. "When he lost at baccarat, he tried taking it out on me, so I sent him back alone."

"You're telling me how you got into the life," he said. "You must really be in love with me."

"Or I'm giving you the same story I gave every other idiot who asked," she said.

"I never asked you."

"Your eyes ask me. Every time they see me. So I took pity and told you. Because you're right. I do love you. More than you're used to, I think."

"I love you too, kid," he said. "But I told you, your share is yours, no strings. If it's money you're after, you don't need me."

"Let's find a place with some humidity," she said. "I'm sick of the desert."

THE END